WHEN WE WERE

young

GEN RYAN

XOXO
Gen
Ryan

For information, contact the publisher, Hot Tree Publishing.
WWW.HOTTREEPUBLISHING.COM

EDITING: HOT TREE EDITING
COVER DESIGNER: CLAIRE SMITH
FORMATTER: RMGRAPHX

ISBN-13: 978-1-925655-27-8

10 9 8 7 6 5 4 3 2 1

MORE FROM GEN RYAN

Thin Red Lines Series
Beautiful Masterpiece (#1)
Beautiful Sacrifice (#2)
Beautiful Torment (#3)

Trade Me Collection (Gay Romance)
Fix You
Losing You

Hopelessly Devoted Series
When We Were Young (#1)
Out of Goodbyes (#2)
More Than Words (#3)

Stand-alone Novels
Three Empty Words

DEDICATION

To anyone, man or woman, who has loved someone so much that you lost parts of yourself. Remember, you have to love yourself first, the rest just falls into place. Know your worth, always. Never let someone tear you apart to the point of losing bits of what makes you who you are. You're worthy of love and kindness, quirks and all.

PROLOGUE

I heard the bell above the door jingle and continued wiping down the table. The diner where I worked was located at a truck stop, so I got decent tips, but this also meant there were tons of creepy men who hadn't seen a woman for God knows how long. That's why I didn't even bother looking up. I figured it was probably a regular who'd sit in their normal spot and holler when they wanted me.

Damn, was I wrong.

"Can I just sit anywhere?" My hand stopped going in mindless circles, and I glanced up—and up and up—before finally landing on two big hazel eyes. He was breathtakingly *broken*. His face and body were slender, not in an athletic way but almost like he hadn't eaten in a while. He had to be well over six feet tall. I wasn't short, but I had to crane my neck to look him in the eyes. He looked at me, a smile curving at the edge of his lips, but it went away just as quick as it appeared. Like a phantom, a hint of what could be.

Happiness.

His face was etched with pain and concern. Furrowed brows and a smile that went away before it took its full shape. I should have run in the other direction, but I was captivated by him.

"Oh, yeah sure! Anywhere's fine," I said a bit too loudly. I watched him walk over to the corner table and pull out the chair, the metal legs scraping against the scarred, damaged floor. He sat down, stretching out his long legs in front of him. I snatched up a menu, pulled down my black apron that did absolutely nothing for my figure, and walked over.

"Here you go." I placed the menu in front of him, and he continued looking down at the table. I wanted his eyes on mine again so I could see the colors of brown that seemed to mirror everything about him.

My mother always said I was a thoughtful child, always looking and analyzing everything. This man intrigued me. Part of me wanted to pull up a chair and ask him questions about why he looked like he had lived his entire life. I knew he couldn't be much older than me, yet he held the weight of the world on his shoulders. It was in the way he hunched over, in his eyes that held so much but never focused on anything. Except mine, albeit briefly. There was something there. The lines on his face that I wanted to trace. Something in me knew that they weren't from old age, but life.

Somehow, I knew it wasn't kind to him. While my life wasn't perfect, his seemed to be far worse, by just the way he carried himself and the clothes that hung off his body. I was intrigued.

"What would you like to drink?" I tapped my foot and tried to shift back to my job and remain professional. This place wasn't professional in the least, but I prided myself on my maturity, so acting like a ditzy teen wasn't in my wheelhouse.

"I'll have a beer and the fish and chips." He picked at his nails and placed his entire order while staring at the table in front of him.

"Wait, you're old enough to have beer?" I leaned in and whispered. Maybe those lines at the corner of his eyes were his age. He let out a laugh that rumbled from his belly and lingered in his throat. I blushed and crossed my arms across my chest, realizing he was joking.

"Kidding. A Coke." Finally, a full smile spread across his face. Gone was the troubled look. The smile made him look like a teenage boy. I let my own smile spread across my lips.

I'd love to make him smile like that every day.

"But I will take the fish and chips," he added.

"Coming right up." I tried to steady myself on my feet when he finally looked at me. Golden speckles swirled in his eyes. At the base of his nose and tops of his cheeks were freckles that brought out his youth even more. He wasn't just breathtakingly broken, he was simply breathtaking. I took a deep breath as I turned on my heels and walked away.

"An order of fish and chips, Jim." I tore the slip out of my pad and hung it where Jim, the cook, could see it.

"You all right?" He raised an eyebrow and motioned to the man sitting in the corner. "You know him?"

"Nope." I pulled down a glass and filled it with ice and Coke.

"You looked at him like you knew him." I pulled a straw out of my apron and tore all of the protective paper off but the top. I jammed it in the glass and looked at Jim. He was old enough to be my father, and when I was here, he always looked out for me.

"Sometimes people just have that impact on you." I shrugged. "It's his eyes," I muttered.

Jim laughed. "Okay there, with your romantic mumbo jumbo." I looked up at him just as he leaned close to me and bulged his eyes. "What about mine. What do you see?"

I giggled and swatted his arm. "A cook who needs to make some fish and chips!" I wiggled my finger at him.

"Right away, ma'am!" He saluted me and headed back further into the kitchen.

Knowing that I had to bring over the drink, I gave myself a little pep talk.

"You can do this. It's just a boy who just happens to make you all mushy inside. You're a teenager. It's natural." Sometimes I had to remind myself that I was a teenage girl and crushing on someone was okay. I didn't typically do normal teenage stuff. I was so focused on my grades and saving my money for college that I didn't party or anything like that. With a nod, I took the soda and made my way back into the seating area. My feet stuck to the floor, and I cursed whoever worked before me and didn't mop. The suctioning sound was like nails on a chalkboard as I walked.

Finally making it to his table, I placed the drink down in front of him.

"Thanks." He ripped off the top of the paper covering the straw and took a long sip. I watched his lips wrap around the straw. His large hands gripped the cup. Was there anything about him that didn't make me want to bat my eyes, twirl my hair, and giggle?

"Everything okay?" He raised his eyebrow, a slight glint in his eye.

And shit, I've been standing here and staring.

"Sorry." I turned to walk away.

Run. Save whatever bit of pride you have left.

"Wait."

I sucked in a breath and turned around.

Ask me my name. My phone number. My astrological sign. Anything.

"Can I get that order to go?" He shuffled in the chair, averting his gaze.

And I scared him away with my creepy staring.

"Absolutely." I put on my best smile and marched

to the kitchen, the sound of my shoes sticking to the floor filling the silence.

"Make that fish and chips to go, Jim." I ripped down a container.

"Easy there, killer." Jim took the container from me, and I glared at him. Jim backed away from me with his hands up in the air. "Just give him your number."

"Why would I do that?" I scrunched up my nose. He was intriguing, sure, but I hadn't ever really dated. I tried it a few times at Ava's—my best friend— push, but no one kept my interest. I was trying to fly through my senior year and go off to college, hoping that somewhere along the way I'd just stumble upon someone who would be it for me. Dating and making small talk? Staying up all night to text, and waiting for phone calls? That wasn't my scene. I stayed up late to read and do homework, not wait on a boy to call me.

"Because." He batted his eyelashes. "His eyes," he said dramatically.

"Oh, shut it!" I finished packing the bag for the order.

I walked over, my feet dragging. I didn't want this stranger to leave. I wasn't accustomed to this, the feeling I had when he spoke to me for the first time. Maybe Jim was right and I should give him my number. Yet I wasn't the type to hand out my number to anyone, or even tell someone I liked them. That was left for Ava. I wasn't shy in the conventional sense; I just hated putting myself out there because that opened the door for rejection.

As I made my way to his table, he stood up, reaching his hand out for the bag.

"Here you go. Enjoy," I said with a perfect smile. He handed me a twenty-dollar bill.

"Keep the change. Thanks again." He turned to walk away.

Don't let him go.

"Wait!" I called out and rummaged through my apron pockets for my pad of paper. Quickly, I scribbled down my name and cell phone number.

"Here. In case you wanted to hang out sometime." I handed him my number, my heart beating erratically in my chest. I was glad I had the apron on, because if not, I was pretty sure he'd be able to see it. He looked down at the paper.

"Rainey," he said. "That name suits you." He didn't say anything else. No promises of calling, or "thanks, here's my name and number too." He left, the door jingling, then slamming behind him.

I looked back at Jim, who shrugged.

With a sigh, I grabbed the mop and pail and started on the floors. I was proud of myself for doing something out of my element. It would likely lead to nothing, but that was okay. I'd stepped out of my comfort zone, and I was proud of myself for that.

CHAPTER ONE

I paced the kitchen floor, each step of my foot heavier than the last. He'd promised me there'd be no more deployments, that he was getting out of the army and we could focus on starting a family and building our life together, which had been in limbo for almost a decade—since that fateful day I laid eyes on him in the diner. I was an idiot to believe him.

He lied. Again. Just like the past four deployments that he volunteered for, he was leaving me behind. The first one I understood, as much as it was difficult to say goodbye. I watched him go with pride as he served his country. Then, he changed. The man I married changed into a stranger, wandering the halls of our home we worked so hard to build, his eyes glossed over, his fists clenched at his sides. I remembered the first time I realized something was slightly off and tried to help him. That was years ago, and things had just gotten worse.

I'd waited a year for Parker. To touch him. To kiss his lips, and I was just moments away from what I'd been dreaming about for months. I looked at myself in the bathroom mirror one last time before heading to the gate.

My palms got sweaty and my mouth went dry. I could feel Parker even before I saw him. It was always that way between us. We were connected on a level that puzzled many people. That's why it was so painful when he left. It was like a part of me was missing.

The door opened and soldiers poured out. People squealed and ran toward them, women and children swept up in a sea of emotions. I stood on my tiptoes to see better over the line of people in front of me. It was always difficult to tell them all apart, but Parker usually stood inches above everyone else. Today was no different.

Our eyes met as soon as he exited the door, and he smiled, the same smile I remembered from the diner, the one that made him look like a young boy. His face was clean-shaven, his hair in a fresh high and tight. Before I could blink, he was in front of me, the emotions of the year causing tears to stream down my face.

"Hey, baby. I missed you." He held my face in his hands, his eyes lingering over my body, the heat swirling around us. When his lips touched mine, everything disappeared. It was just us, no one else. Gone were the noises of other families reuniting.

9

"I've been waiting a year to do that," I whispered against his mouth.

"I've been waiting to do a lot more than that." Parker's eyes danced with excitement as his licked his lips. *"Let's get out of here. All I can think about is getting you out of that dress."* Hand in hand, we made our way out of the airport.

I was on cloud nine. Nothing could taint the way I felt. When we got home, we barely made it into the house before his hands were up my dress. Kneeling in front of me, he slowly lifted the skirt.

"Fuck, Rainey, you aren't wearing any underwear." He looked up at me, and I winked.

"Easy access. I didn't want you to have to work for it today."

Parker stood up and looked me straight in the eyes. Whenever he did this, it was so intense, because he'd had trouble making eye contact since I met him. The emotion that was inside of him, the struggles and pain, all stayed in his eyes.

"I'll always work for you. I'll always fight for you. Without you, there's nothing worth fighting for." There was a loud knock at the door, and Parker rolled on the ground, pulling me down with him. My entire body jerked, then slammed against the hardwood floor.

"Stay down!" he yelled, shielding my head with his body. I looked up at my husband; his eyes were dark and filled with such fear, hate, and rage that I gasped.

"Parker, baby." I reached out and touched his

cheek, just as another knock came at the door. "You're home. There's nothing to be afraid of anymore."

After a few blinks, Parker stood up and stormed off, leaving me alone on the cool, bare floor. I stayed there for a minute, trying to gather my bearings. What just happened? Then reality hit me. My husband may have come back from the war, but parts of him had been left behind. Parts that I may never get back.

I knew the signs of PTSD. It was something I had become familiar with, especially after doing a rotation at the VA during my clinicals at nursing school. Parker didn't want to hear it though. He knew he needed help, but refused. So instead, he signed up to deploy as often as he could. It was easier to be in the shit than at home.

I promised to stick by him through sickness and in health, but it got harder as each day trudged along and he chose death and destruction, his mind slowly becoming deeper and deeper entrenched in war. Sometimes I felt like he was choosing those things over me. Over a life that held so much happiness and promise. Kids. A home. Stability. How was that supposed to make anyone feel? Not loved or cared for. After eight years of marriage, I felt like a burden, and that maybe the man I loved was too far gone.

I heard his truck pull into the driveway, and sat at the kitchen table and waited. I couldn't keep my feelings bottled up anymore. If there was any hope for our marriage, we needed to communicate. Something that had fallen by the wayside years before. We were more like friends passing in the breeze. He needed something, I got it, often before he even asked.

"Hey," Parker mumbled as he threw his things on the counter and typed out a quick text. He'd been spending more time on his phone lately, wrapped up in something that I couldn't figure out. He had received a promotion at work, so I assumed that the excessive phone use was because of his new position. All I knew was that it took him forever to text me back, yet his phone was always in his hand. Walking right past without so much as a kiss or a hug, he opened the fridge and pulled out a beer.

"We need to talk," I said as convincingly as possible. My voice shook, because despite my confidence in certain aspects of my life, like my career as a nurse, I lacked it in almost every other area. I loved Parker, but upsetting him terrified me. He never hit me, but his anger only increased as each day passed. Maybe it was just his tolerance for me. I think that's what scared me. That he tolerated me. That I was simply here because it was convenient. I didn't want to know the truth behind how he really felt about me, so I buried it for many years.

I couldn't take it anymore. Parts of me were dying slowly, disappearing before my eyes. I had tried to help Parker, but the cost was becoming increasingly higher as each day went on. I was losing myself.

"Oh, for fuck's sake, Rainey. I just got home, lay off, will you?" His phone dinged, and he smiled and shoved it back in his pocket. My heart twisted in my chest. I couldn't remember the last time he smiled like that, at least not at me.

I cringed at his words and took a deep breath, digging around within my broken self for any resolve I had left. I couldn't let this slide anymore. He needed to know.

"Sit, Parker. I'm not kidding." I looked up at him, tears glistening in my eyes. He roughly pulled out the chair, the legs rubbing against the floor.

We stared at each other for what seemed like forever, our unspoken words saying more than anything I could ever voice. His look was pure disgust, dripping with disdain as my tears fell.

"I'm guessing you found out I'm leaving again. So, who told you this time?" Parker asked, taking a pull of his beer.

"Leslie next door. She asked me how I felt about you leaving next week for Afghanistan." Tears streamed down my face, and I quickly wiped them away. "You can imagine my shock when she told me my husband was leaving for a year in just a few days, and I knew nothing about it."

Parker hung his head and, for a second, looked like the man I married so many years ago. A man who cared about how I was doing and walked miles to bring me soup and flowers when I was sick with the flu in high school. I reached out and took his hand in mine to seek comfort, like I used to. As quickly as my old Parker was there, he was gone, the anger, the hatred taking him over. He jerked his hand away.

"I knew you'd be pissed I signed up. I didn't want to hear it. The guilt." He let out his breath and stood up, polished off his beer, and threw it in the recycling.

"The guilt?" I laughed between the tears. "The guilt of what? You obviously don't care that you're leaving me again. You don't have to go! You keep signing up, and here I am left to live this life that is supposed to be ours." I shook my head. "It isn't ours. It's a shit life where I pretend each day when you walk out that door that it doesn't kill me that you need them more than you need me!" I was screaming, full-fledged shaking and crying, standing in front of the man that was once my everything. When did he become anything less? There was something about getting older that put things into perspective. Made you think about what it was that you wanted out of life. I guess it was that bigger picture that everyone talked about. I thought my bigger picture was crystal clear, but I had always been staring through chipped glass, and now it was shattering. I couldn't see anything but a distorted image of myself.

"They understand." Parker moved toward me, taking my face in his hands. Using his thumb, he wiped a tear from my cheek. "They get me. They know what it's like," he whispered.

There were times like this, when a simple touch brought me back to the way things were. How gentle he could be when there was nothing but love between us. Now there were wars and years spent apart. There was distance.

"I got you once. Remember?" I smiled at the memories of us finishing each other's sentences and spending every second we could together. Now, we passed in own our home, like strangers. I breathed in deeply, taking in the scent of him. He always smelled the same, like Irish Spring. Since I met him, that's all he'd ever used to shower. It was clean, fresh, and alive. A direct contrast to how I knew he felt. Sometimes, he'd give me snippets of what was going on in his head. That's what kept me going, those moments of honesty and truth. Deep down, the Parker I married was in there, struggling to break free.

Parker stepped back, snatched his wallet and keys from the counter, and headed toward the door. He turned back and looked at me, clutching the doorknob in his hand. "That was then. This is now. I'm going to war again because that's all I am now. A soldier." The door slammed, shaking the pictures of us that lined the walls.

Falling to the ground, I cried. This wasn't what my life was supposed to be. I'd had it all planned, and nowhere along the way did meeting Parker and falling madly in love at only seventeen fall into that plan. But life had a funny way of flipping the script, taking all your plans and throwing them out the window. I crashed and burned long ago. Parker and I both had.

We were holding on to this marriage for what? I loved the old him, who left years ago. I'd thought maybe I could bring him back by loving him more, giving him more. I knew that was crazy thinking, yet I couldn't walk away. I didn't want to give up on him. He needed someone, and I was all he had.

The sad thing was, I'd always known I loved him more than he loved me, and that had been okay. But now, something in me wanted more. I wanted to be loved with such a passion that I couldn't breathe. That when he looked at me, I couldn't help but smile no matter how shitty my day was. When Parker looked at me now, all I saw was disdain, a man filled with regret. I couldn't be his regret anymore. I deserved more, and that was absolutely terrifying.

CHAPTER TWO

It was a feeling I'd never wish on my worst enemy: heartache. It felt like being dangled over the edge of a cliff and knowing if the person let go, you'd fall to your death. The anticipation, though, the hanging and waiting for them to release you, that was the worst part. The unknown, the fear. That's what heartache was like. There was never a thought that someone else could come along and make me forget about my love for Parker. I never so much as thought of another guy. I put my all into our marriage, with the hope that maybe the person I loved would realize what he had in front of him.

Reality was, I was alone.

Always.

Despite my anger with Parker for signing up for another deployment, we worked as a team tonight, packing up his duffle bags and footlocker, filling it with his life. Sad thing was, his life fit in those bags and footlockers. It was filled with clothes, army gear, and whatever other items meant something to him. As I folded another green T-shirt, I let the tears fall. Despite everything, I was sad to see him go, but for the first time, I realized I wasn't his life. Maybe I never had been.

"Babe." Parker wrapped his arms around me and rested his chin on my head. "It's going to be all right." I looked up at him as I often did, my eyes pleading with him to understand me. Every time I looked at Parker, I was transported back to the first day I saw him at the diner. I held on to that memory. It kept me going; it gave me hope. Looking up at him now, all I saw was loneliness, a lifetime of me hoping he would choose me, settle down and start a family. I would never ask him to give up what he loved for me, though. I couldn't help but think if he loved me, he would have already chosen me and I wouldn't even have to ask.

The doubt crept up like the sly bastard that it was, and I opened my mouth to disagree. His lips crashed down on mine before I could say anything. Sex with Parker was never slow or sensual; it was always filled with need. Hands grasping like it was the last time we'd ever touch, biting and clawing. It was the only time lately I was connected to him, and that's what I needed now. To feel whatever there was left of him. Of us.

I grasped his shoulders, my fingers digging in to his

hard muscles. Parker lived at the gym, so every inch of him that was once slender had been replaced with solid muscle. He wasn't overly muscular, but extremely fit. I liked looking down at his massive chest as I rode him till he came. He had become a gorgeous man, matured from the young boy I fell in love with.

He threw me down on the bed; his bags fell to the ground, spilling out all our hard work. Neither of us cared, we were too worried about shedding all the clothes that separated us. There was so much more between us than clothes, but here, now, we were all that mattered. It was times like this I was thankful for having an IUD. No need to stop and worry about condoms or anything else.

With one gyration of his hips, he entered me, causing my head to roll back in pleasure. Parker stretched me out each time, his width and massive length filling me to the brim.

Each thrust brought me closer and closer to the edge that I'd been dangling over for months. I held on as long as I could, our slick bodies molding together until I couldn't hang on anymore. Everything crashed around me, like waves I couldn't control. I screamed in ecstasy before everything hit me.

I was tired of being strong and pushing back the frustration and fear that my marriage was over. Every day I smiled and tried damn hard to bring things back to where they were. But people changed. Getting married so young had shocked our families. To us, love was love; whether we were eighteen or thirty-five, we just knew that what we had was real. I hadn't thought about time, though, that fickle little bitch that held everyone hostage and changed whatever she damn well pleased. Time ruined us. Time apart and at war. Distance had always been our enemy.

Parker slid out of me, and I bit my bottom lip in an effort to not cry out as each memory battered me.

"Hey. You okay?" With his arms on either side of me, he hovered over me.

"Please. Don't go," I choked out.

Stay with me. Choose me.

These were all common feelings I had before he left, wanting to get down on my knees and beg him to stay. Tonight, I saw red. Why was I begging a man who clearly had no concern for me, no thought for how I'd fare if he left again? I sat up, pushing him aside. I was still semidressed, but I didn't give a flying fuck.

"Why, Parker? Why did you sign up again? We were supposed to start a family. Settle down and actually start our life together without having to say goodbye all the time." The tears kept streaming as he stared at me, baffled by my honesty.

He knelt in front of me, his vulnerability taking me off guard. Now at my eye level, he looked at me, his eyes glistening with tears.

"Because I don't deserve this life." He reached out and caressed my cheek. "I don't deserve you or this house." He shook his head as he removed his hand.

"I need the adrenaline. The pain of running off into the shit and trying to survive. That's all I did my entire life before I met you, I survived."

So much of his life was just surviving before we met. He was homeless at the age of seventeen, living with whatever family or friends would let him crash for a while. His sister, Emily, was pregnant, using drugs, and a dropout all by the age of sixteen. We were so different, but I thought love had to be enough. Because it always was, wasn't it?

I grabbed his shoulders and brought him close to me, holding him tight against my chest. We stayed like that for what seemed like forever, listening to each other breathe, feeling the rise and fall of each other's chest. I knew now why he left. I also knew that no matter what I did, I couldn't be what he needed me to be. I didn't have to just survive growing up. Our differences back then were what drew us together, that despite his shitty childhood he was able to show me such kindness and love. That was the type of man that I wanted to spend the rest of my life with. War, though, changed a man. It took a kind soul and ripped him in two and brought him to his knees. It brought up his past, made it his present, and left behind those he loved and those who loved him in the process. Our life, our future, didn't make sense anymore.

As Parker kneeled before me, cradled in my arms, I feared for the first time that we might not make it. That we were broken beyond repair.

CHAPTER THREE

It was a place I'd been many times before, standing with weeping families as they clung to their soldier for dear life. I learned over the years and multiple deployments that no matter how tightly I clung to Parker, he'd still leave and I'd still be left here alone.

Parker and I sat side by side on the bleachers, our elbows the only part of us touching. Around us everyone wept and made promises of waiting forever, talking every day on the phone, and writing daily. Little did they know that what awaited them was sleepless nights, staring at their phone and computer waiting for a call, and letters that came less and less as the deployment waned on.

There were times I didn't know whether Parker would make it home. I tried to avoid the news stations, but my sister-in-law, Emily, used to make it her mission to text or call me with every mention of an area remotely close to his. I lived in constant fear and agony, a shell of a person, because my heart lived outside of my chest—a part of it anyway. Parker always took it with him, wherever he went.

"Sergeant?" A young soldier I didn't recognize stood in front of us at parade rest. "The commander said we're getting ready to head out." I took a deep breath as Parker nodded.

"Well." Parker stood up and straightened his uniform. "I guess I better go."

The familiar lump in my throat formed and the walls seemed to cave in around me. There was something so final about this goodbye. The air held an aura that wasn't filled with the same familiar heartache. It clung to me, like wet clothes, dragging me down. This was it.

"Walk me out, Rainey?" He held out his hand for me. "Please, like we used to?" I closed my eyes and thought of the first deployment. How I held his hand until the absolute last minute. How he kissed me with such force and conviction. It was the kiss I held on to for the entire year he was gone. I wanted that again, to have the comfort of his lips against mine and have that memory restored.

I slipped my hand in his, and we walked in silence. No matter how hard we tried, things would never be the way they used to. When we were young, we had our entire lives ahead of us. Open hearts, free spirits. Now, plagued with war and hate, years apart and life that hadn't always been kind, that youth, the freedom and hope, washed away long ago. All we were left with was distant memories of times when there was love.

We stopped in front of the bus that would take Parker and his soldiers to their plane. They were all piling on and waving to their loved ones. Parker and I were among the last ones to say goodbye.

I watched as a female soldier walked by and eyeballed us. I gave her a small smile, but she scowled and walked away. Parker squeezed my hand and redirected my attention.

"Will you wait for me?" His eyes were filled with the confusion and uncertainty that I too felt down to my core. He searched my face for my answer, but I didn't know. Would I wait for him? Could I put the life I'd been promised on hold for another year while he chased whatever it was he needed? I wanted to say yes. That like all the other times, I'd be here. I'd send him packages and be ready for every call and Skype date that he wanted. But something in me this time wasn't so sure. I loved Parker. He'd made me realize that there was more to life than books, school, and grades. Sometimes though, all I wanted was simple. A life where I didn't have to worry about whether I'd be a widow before my thirtieth birthday. The price for that life, though, was not having his corny jokes, or him leaving the toilet seat up and his dirty laundry strewn all over the house. I didn't know if I could live without those little things. I didn't know if I could live without him.

"Rainey?" I crashed my lips down on his, willing those feelings of hope and love to swirl around with our interlacing tongues. Butterflies formed in my stomach, flitting with the anticipation of his departure.

Whistles filled the air, and I blushed at my display of affection. We separated, albeit reluctantly, panting with the passion that was felt in just those few seconds. It wasn't hope that lingered in my mind, but dread that maybe this was it for us.

I trembled through the tears that were freely falling. I couldn't find the words I wanted to say, because honestly, I didn't know what I wanted.

Leaning in, I kissed Parker on the cheek. "Let me know when you make it there safely. I'll always be there for you."

He smiled that crooked grin that sent shivers down my spine even to this day.

My lips curved up slightly, and Parker chuckled at my attempt to try to remain solemn.

"You still love me," he said wistfully.

I took his face in my hands and stared at him with such intensity that his breath stopped.

"I'll always love you, Parker."

He leaned in and kissed me softly. "I'll always love you too."

I waved as they drove away. I stood tall, wiping away a few stray tears as everyone else around me wept and huddled together. I was alone, my arms wrapped around myself for whatever comfort I could gather from my own arms.

"Are you okay, sweetie?" An older woman stood next to me and placed her hand on my shoulder. I smiled big and nodded.

"It's okay to not be okay. It's okay to cry." I didn't know who this woman was, but I was tired of being strong, composed, and thoughtful. She brought me close against her chest, and I bawled like a baby, just like the first time he left. I was brought back to all those years ago when I said goodbye for the first time, and the pain was as real as it was that day. Now, the difference was, I wasn't sure whether he loved me anymore or if I'd just become a common thing in his life, like getting up and brushing your teeth. This woman thought I was crying for my husband, and I was, but not because he was going off to war; it was deeper than that. I was crying for my marriage. I was crying for a life that never quite became what it should have.

CHAPTER FOUR

"Are you sure you're okay?" Ava, my best friend since high school, my rock, my voice of reason, had called me every day for the past three weeks since Parker left. Every night ended with the same question. Was I okay?

That's such a weird question, considering "okay" was rather relative. Parker still hadn't called me. I'd gotten a few emails, some missed messages on Skype, but I'd been working and trying to keep going without falling into the common theme that deployments brought for me.

Depression.

It's something I'd suffered from since adolescence, and living the military life hadn't made it much easier. I threw myself into work and school and anything else I could to try to fill the void that Parker left. With the way we left things, I was even more gutted. I knew that considering divorce or separation was for the best, but when someone was your entire life, it still hurt.

"I'm fine. I promise." I poured my coffee into my mug and sealed it off. Checking my bag to make sure it was packed with my lunch and dinner, I headed out for my twelve-hour shift at the hospital.

"I'm a plane ride away." She laughed. "Don't make me bring myself and my three kids all the way down to North Carolina."

I laughed, although a visit from Ava and all her children would be amazing. "You're the best," I said as I started my car.

"I know." A loud thump and a cry vibrated through the phone. "Shit," Ava muttered. "I got to go, hon. I love you and do what's best for you. You deserve to be happy. Even if that means moving on. Sometimes things aren't meant to last forever. You tried your best. Gave it your all." There was a pause. "Holy shit, Amelia, what did you do?" I sniffed and wiped the tears away.

"I love you."

"Love you, girl. Chat soon." I was left with what I'd known deep down all along. Everything was in my control. It always had been. I could move on and live life, or continue to hope that Parker would come around and that he'd realize that my love for him was so strong and I'd do anything to make him happy. The question was whether he'd do everything for me?

***

The night at work started off slow enough, which was unheard of as an ER nurse. I was usually running from place to place with emergency after emergency. I actually got to eat the dinner I packed tonight.

"Rainey!" My coworker Melissa ran down the hall with a cart. "Teenage gunshot victim, ETA two minutes." I ran toward her, the adrenaline flowing through my veins. It wasn't subtle. It was intense, coursing through me and giving me laser focus. This was what I lived for, where I was in my element. Parker had said he felt the same at war. The difference was I never left him behind. I chose this career so I could start a family. Build the home I so badly wanted with him. He chose to leave when I wanted him to stay.

We waited at the emergency room doors, the sound of the incoming ambulance deafening. I swayed from leg to leg as the kid was rushed out of the back of the ambulance and into the hospital.

"Gunshot to the right side. Extreme loss of blood." I took in all the information as Melissa and I went to work. We stabilized him enough that the bleeding stopped, and he was whisked to surgery.

Everything started to die down. The adrenaline melted away, and I was left with the aftermath of a trauma. As I cleaned the blood from my hands, I felt confident, in control, powerful. As a calmness came over me, I couldn't help but realize how much I loved my job.

"Great work out there. You sure you aren't a doctor?" I turned around and saw the paramedic leaning against the doorframe. I laughed and dried my hands.

"My student loans are horrific enough. I'd be scared to see what they'd look like for a doctor." He laughed. It was deep and traveled through me, sending shivers down my spine. I shook it off and chalked it up to frazzled nerves.

"Cold? They do keep these hospitals pretty chilly." He walked into the room and held out his hand. "I'm Levi, by the way."

Shaking his hand, I replied, "Rainey."

"That's an interesting name." He smiled and cocked his head to the side, studying me a bit more.

"My mom liked the rain," I added. For some reason, I was feeling funny. I needed a good laugh.

He laughed for what seemed like forever. I remained stoic and serious, my face never showing that I was joking.

"Oh shit." He squared his shoulders. "You're serious?"

"Yes. I'm serious. My sister's name is Snow."

He shook his head nervously. "I'm sorry. I'm an asshole." He ran his fingers through his light brown hair. I stared at it for longer than necessary; the loose curls highlighted his chiseled features. He had a beard, which I normally didn't care for but suited him, close-cut and tight to his cheeks and chin. He had to be only a couple inches taller than me because I didn't need to crane my neck to look up at him.

"I'm kidding." I laughed. "My mom liked the name, and I'm an only child."

He let out his breath. "Jesus. I thought I was batting a thousand on my first impression. Way to impress the ladies."

I gulped at his response. He was trying to impress me? The banter back and forth was harmless, but guilt spurred in me and I thought about Parker. Although things were still left in limbo between us, I drew the line at innocent flirting.

"I've got to get back to work." I slid past him, purposely trying not to touch him. "Nice to meet you."

I rushed down the hall before he could respond.

"Raindrop!" he called after me as he hustled to catch up. I grinned to myself at the nickname. "I hope you didn't take offense to anything I said back there. I was trying to be funny." He ran his fingers through his hair again. "Which isn't really my strong suit," he mumbled.

Okay. I was overreacting. He wasn't asking me out or doing anything inappropriate. Other than a few coworkers here, I didn't have many friends. Ava was about it, and a few army wives I was forced into relationships with. It kind of came with the territory.

"No. You're fine." Awkwardness swarmed around us. I glanced down at my phone. "This is usually when my husband emails me or gets on Skype. I don't want to miss him." *That's right. Mention Parker. Your husband. Lay it all out there so there's no funny business. Even though he hasn't called you in days.*

"Husband?" I caught a hint of disappointment. "How long have you been married?" he asked.

"Eight years," I said as I clutched my phone. I knew Parker wouldn't call me, but holding my phone made me feel safe and connected to him.

"Wow. So, what, you got married as an infant?"

I smiled. Levi's jokes really were horrible. "No, when I was eighteen. He's in the military."

"Ah." Levi nodded. "You guys are one of those."

My back went stiff. "What does that mean?"

He shrugged, and then his eyes got large. "I didn't mean anything…."

"No. You don't know me, Levi." I moved closer to him and pressed my finger against his chest. "You think you know why I married my husband at eighteen, because of some stereotype?" He opened his mouth to respond, and I shook my head. "Don't bother trying to explain yourself. Sure, my marriage isn't all rainbows and butterflies, but what marriage is? Yes, I got married at eighteen, but it wasn't for extra money in the paycheck or some other stereotypical army family bullshit story. We loved each other."

Levi put up his hands. "Listen. I honestly didn't mean anything by it. I give you credit for staying married. My marriage lasted six months before my wife slept around on me." I loosened up a bit at his confusion. "Some women can't hack the man who works and is away from home for too long. I was in the army for four years. I know how it can be."

"It's a difficult life, but I don't regret it." The words sounded flat because I wasn't sure if I meant it anymore, but this stranger in front of me didn't need to know that.

Levi's pager sounded, and he glanced down. "Duty calls."

"Yeah," I said. Levi turned on his heels and walked away, and I headed in the other direction. Shaking my head, I felt like an asshole.

"Rainey?" I turned to face Levi one last time. "Just remember you said that you guys loved each other." And with that, he was gone.

It was true. I'd said we loved each other. Not that we were in love with each other.

As if sensing my turmoil, my phone vibrated in my hand with an incoming email from Parker. Pulling it up, I took a minute to read it.

Rainey,

I won't be available for a while. Going on a long mission without access to Internet or phones.

I needed reassurance, and this email didn't help my already whirling mind with the doubt that plagued it. I heard my name being called and saw people running toward the ambulance bay. Shoving my phone in my pocket, I refocused on my job, because that was the only constant that I had right now. My work and Ava. Everything else was in limbo.

CHAPTER FIVE

"So, you're telling me some random guy you never met before convinced you of something I've been trying to convince you of for years?"

"It's not that easy, Ava." I sighed.

"Was he hot at least?" She laughed, and I stayed silent. "He was hot, wasn't he?"

"Okay!" I scolded. "Levi's hotness had nothing to do with me realizing that I'm ready to move on, I think." I tried my best to sound convincing, but my words alarmed even me. I wasn't in the right mindset, so I'd probably find Santa Claus attractive right now.

"Sure. Whatever you say," Ava scoffed.

"I'm not a damn hussy!"

"Obviously, I know this." Ava paused. "What are you going to do?"

I leaned back on the couch and stared at the ceiling.

"I have no idea. I don't want to have this conversation

with him via email while he's fighting to stay alive. A Dear John letter sounds pretty shitty."

"Yeah," Ava agreed. "But you both kind of left it on ending terms. So now you should wait a year to start living? I know you, Rainey, you won't even look at another guy until it's official," she lectured.

"I don't even care about other men. I just want to be happy." My heart twisted in my chest. I was happy once, when we were in high school and life seemed so simple.

"And happy you shall be!" Ava professed as call waiting beeped.

"A private number's calling through. I better get it."

Ava sighed. "I'll hold. Kids are napping, thank Christ." I clicked over.

"Hello?"

"Hey." Parker's voice sounded distorted and distant as it rang through my ears. I stumbled on my words at the realization that it was him.

I wasn't expecting him to call. Quite frankly, he never called, even when times were good. I was always here. No effort was needed to keep me waiting all these years. I was here whenever he needed me. Maybe that was my problem? Making myself so easily attainable and accessible. *Little late to realize that.*

"Is everything okay?" My senses were on alert, thinking about what could be going on that he needed to call me.

"Everything's fine. I wanted to talk to you about something." My shoulders went rigid. That was never a good start to a conversation.

"Okay." I sat down because I knew this was going to be it. The moment that I knew was coming. The end.

"I've met someone." My throat went dry. That wasn't what I was expecting at all. Never once had the possibility that he had met someone crossed my mind. Then it all clicked. The text messaging. The smiling. The fucking girl eyeballing me.

"How long?" Something in me knew that this was a while in the making. I wanted to be angry, but my insecurity crept in. I wanted to punch him, call him every name in the book, but I wanted the facts. To know how dumb I'd been and for how long.

"Does it matter?" Back was his tone that always got under my skin but caused me to shut my mouth without question. Not this time. I wouldn't cower and nod and accept what he said. I was fiercely loyal, had altered my entire life to suit his. I at least deserved to know what the fuck had been going on while I'd been trying to keep our marriage together.

"It matters!" I screamed, not recognizing my own voice. I was shaking, my entire body pulsing with the anger that coursed through me. I felt betrayed and completely stupid. I had given my entire life to this man, not long ago felt his lips against mine, and those same lips had been on someone else's. "Do you remember when we saw each other after we met for the first time in the diner and you made up that poem?" I closed my eyes and remembered how special I'd felt. I didn't feel special anymore. I felt used and discarded.

I'd been a fucking idiot to think that Parker loved me still.

All eyes were on me as I walked to the front of the classroom and pulled out the roster the teacher had given me. Mrs. Mulligan was my favorite teacher. My AP English Literature and creative writing teacher and mentor. Since I'd finished all my English requirements for graduation, plus aced my AP exam, the principal agreed to let me be a teaching assistant.

I knew all the students on the roster except one, Parker Matthews. I glanced around for an unfamiliar face and didn't see anyone. Shrugging, I placed the paper down to get the class started for Mrs. Mulligan.

"All right, who has an original work that they are ready to share?" I had hated the first time Mrs. Mulligan asked my class to share our work. I wasn't a writer. I had never cared for it really, but I loved reading, literature, how someone could string words together and make you feel whatever they wanted. I was envious of that power. I'd tried, repeatedly, but my structured mind never let me go anywhere beyond prose that sounded like something out of The Cat and the Hat. *Mrs. Mulligan was kind, though, and never gave up on me.*

"No one?" I glanced around at the red faces. "Okay, I guess I'll have to pick someone." Walking up and down the aisles, I paused just as the door to the classroom opened. Like a cool breeze, the body, the face, the walk I remembered from that night at the

diner stood before me. Looking me straight in the eyes, he found the only empty seat and placed his bag on the ground before sliding his long frame into the seat.

Girls whispered and giggled, causing my cheeks to flush at the realization that I wasn't the only one who found him captivating. I wanted to stake my claim, but he wasn't mine. Hell, he'd never even called me.

I couldn't move or find my voice, which seemed to have left once he entered the room. My mouth opened, then shut, and more giggles filled the air.

"Share your original work, Mr. Matthews." Mrs. Mulligan entered and nodded to me as she went to the front of the room.

I tried to will my eyes to not follow him as he walked past me. He faced the class, giving the grin that had made me think about him all summer with just one encounter.

He cleared his throat, then began.

"Her voice was like satin, smooth against my warm skin. Each curve of her body visible beneath the black apron that clung to parts of her that she hid from the world. But I'm no stranger to hiding parts that you hate. I saw right through her, to the woman—the perfection—that was underneath."

I clutched the side of a desk, my mouth hanging open as Mrs. Mulligan looked between him and me. A smile crept on her lips.

"Seems we have a romantic in here, ladies." More whispers flowed through the room. "Thank you for

sharing, Parker. You may have a seat." He passed right by me, the row between the desks seeming too small for us both to fit. Sucking in my stomach, I inhaled, the soft scent of Irish Spring wafting around me.

"Rainey," he whispered as he scooted by. And with just the sound of my name, everything Ava had been saying to me came into my mind. Live. Be a teenager. I wanted him. His words, his mouth that said my name like it was the sweetest thing that ever graced his lips. Whether that poem was something he wrote months ago when we first met, or made up from just seeing me now, he remembered me, and damn, did I remember him.

Those were the days that I wanted to remember fondly. The times when there were no struggles between us, when we were just getting to know each other. When we were young.

"We were young, Rainey. Things are different now."

I chuckled. "Yeah, because you've stuck your dick into someone else. What does she have that I don't?" My insecurities crept in, and I hated it. I stared down at my wide hips and slight pouch of my stomach. Maybe if I was skinnier, fitter. I shook my head to rid myself of those thoughts. This wasn't my fault. No matter what flaws I had, no one deserved to be cheated on.

"Don't go there. I'm not going to tell you who she is or compare the two of you. You'll always be my first love. But that's the thing about first loves, they aren't always meant to last forever."

I was dumbfounded. Had I spent my entire life forcing something that was doomed from the start? The high school sweethearts that people said were so strong and so much in love, when really our marriage was slowly dying as each day went on? Parker was right. They weren't made to last forever. At least ours wasn't.

I chest and stared. Where the hell did I go from here?

CHAPTER SIX

Another day, another dollar. I kept replaying the conversation between Parker and me through my mind. There was nothing left. My marriage was over and my effort was for shit. There's nothing like knowing you'd been trying to keep things together when your husband had been trying to find his happiness elsewhere. I guess I wasn't worth the effort, and that fucking sucked to realize.

"Hey, Raindrop." Levi stood at the nurses' station grinning ear to ear. In his hands were two steaming cups of coffee, and I swear I drooled at the smell of the fresh beans wafting to my nose. I let out a moan.

I had seen Levi in passing a few times since our last exchange. We were cordial, but something about him put me on edge. He was a good guy, I could feel it. But my current state of mind left me in jeopardy of making poor decisions. And Levi was a bad decision waiting to happen.

"If I knew the key to your heart was coffee, I would have started sooner." He placed the cup in my hand, and I brought it to my lips and closed my eyes, relishing the liquid's smoothness as it slid down my throat. Coffee gave me life. Crazy, but it did, and this coffee was everything.

"How'd you know how I like it?" I whispered, holding the cup between my hands. I hadn't spoken to him since that day I laid into him. Nothing like coffee to heal one's soul and mend broken fences.

"Jean told me." I should have said something about him asking how I liked my coffee, but I didn't care. Right now, I needed the coffee, especially since it was only 12:00 a.m. and I was here until seven.

"How's your husband?" he asked between sips of his coffee. I was taken aback by him asking and nearly choked.

"Parker's okay. We got to talk briefly a few nights ago." I coughed and tried to avoid Levi's eyes as I spoke about Parker. I didn't want to tell him that I was getting a divorce. That I had no clue where my life was headed. But God, did I want to bare my soul to this complete stranger. He just made me comfortable, even when everything else in my life was going to shit.

"That's good. Communication is key during deployment. It's hard, but—"

"Levi! Rainey!" Jean came to the nurses' station and leaned against it. "Tomorrow night we are going to the Rusty Saloon for some drinks and appetizers. You two are invited."

"Oh, I don't usually go out." I put my cup of coffee down and continued charting.

Jean shook her head. "Right." She turned to Levi. "I've been trying to get her to go out for years, and she always turns us down."

"Is that so?" Levi seemed amused as he looked between Jean and me.

"I'll think about it. I'm very busy." I took another sip of my coffee and tried to focus on the charting in front of me. I had no plans, other than my pajamas, takeout, and Netflix. That was my idea of a good time.

"Busy. Right." Jean laughed. "I'm off to cuddle the babies!" she said in a singsong way as she nearly skipped down the hall. Jean worked in the maternity ward and adored the babies. I adored babies too and would sneak up there on breaks and hold them. I wanted to be a mother so bad. Parker wasn't sure he wanted kids.

Now, I was even further away from being a mother. Nothing like going backward in life.

"You don't have any plans, do you?" Levi raised his eyebrow.

"I like to just relax at home. You know this type of work can wear you out." I didn't make eye contact with Levi, but I could feel his eyes boring into me.

"You wait for him to call. Sit at home and hold the phone in your hands." My head shot up. "My ex-wife used to do that. She said that's what drew her to find someone else. She hated waiting. It drove her mad." He let out a small laugh. "So instead of finding balance in her life, she cheated."

"I'm not a cheater." I placed down my coffee a little too hard, spilling some of it over the top of the cup. I hardly knew Levi at all, so the thought of sharing with him that Parker had moved on and that my marriage was over seemed a bit odd, but it was on the tip of my tongue to prove to him that I wasn't the one who'd stepped out on my marriage.

"I'm sure you aren't. But neither was Heather, my ex. Deployments wreak havoc on relationships if not handled with care. You sitting at home isn't healthy. I'm sure Parker wouldn't want that."

I hated that he was right. I knew my obsession with waiting and never missing a call or email wasn't healthy. I felt bad going out and having a good time while Parker was in Afghanistan and I didn't know if he was cold, fighting off gunfire, or had a place to lay his head. If he was miserable, I thought I had to be miserable.

I guess none of that mattered anymore, did it?

"I felt bad. Having fun."

Levi's eyes softened. "Come out with us tomorrow. Just for a bit. It's okay to live your life. Your marriage will be better for it."

My marriage is over. He has someone else, and I'm all alone.

"Why do you just show up and drop emotional bombshells on me?" I shook my head. "You're some evil mastermind."

Levi laughed. "Just know what it's like, that's all." He leaned over the counter, his uniform tautening against his body "What do you say?"

"I'll think about it." I grinned. "Now, don't you have people to save?"

Levi laughed as he walked away, leaving me to focus on my charting and relish the few seconds that the ER wasn't crazy busy. I didn't know where life was headed for me, but for the first time in a while, I smiled, and I meant it.

CHAPTER SEVEN

I refused to wallow in my own self-pity, although curling up in my bed with a carton of Ben and Jerry's sounded like a much better idea than having to be dressed in actual clothes and go out. I pulled my covers over my head. If you can't see anything, it doesn't exist, right?

I listened to *The Notebook* playing in the background, resisting the urge to chuck my ice-cream carton at the TV screen. It was all a lie. Romance. Love. The happily ever after. I felt another crying session coming on and buried myself further into my bed. I was safe here.

My phone dinged, and I groaned, fumbling outside the blanket to grab it. I squinted to read the message.

Ava: Put the Ben and Jerry's down. Get dressed and try to have a good time.

I smiled and typed out a quick reply. I loved that Ava and I had such a great relationship to the point where she knew exactly what I would be doing even without me having to tell her. I rolled out of bed, my head spinning from all the crying. Looking at myself in the mirror, my puffy eyes and tearstained cheeks made me laugh.

"God, I'm ridiculous." I shook my head at my reflection.

"The best kind of love is the kind that...." Those words from *The Notebook* made me scoff. There was no best kind of love. There's the kind that knocked someone over and made them forget who the hell they were. The kind that caused people to lose themselves in someone who couldn't give two shits, who fell in love with someone else and gave an excuse that the other person deserved better. It was all a load of horseshit, because I deserved not to be cheated on when I put my all into my marriage. All I had to show for it was low self-esteem and an empty carton of Ben and Jerry's Coffee, Coffee, Buzz, Buzz.

After a quick shower, I threw on a pair of jeans and a flowy top that was dressy enough to look like I put in an effort. Hell, it was better than the ripped yoga pants and stained T-shirt I'd been wearing before. I then headed out.

***

I stood outside the bar and stared inside as all my coworkers laughed and had fun. I was sure I resembled some sort of crazy stalker looking longingly inside with a scowl on my face that could make a grown man cry. Everyone was laughing, dancing, and happy. I wasn't. It felt wrong going in there and pretending. My face was getting sore from fake smiling.

"Are you going to just stand outside or are you going to go in?" I turned around and saw Levi, his normal paramedic uniform replaced with jeans and a plain white T-shirt.

"Probably just going to stand out here and pretend that I'm not ready to have a meltdown at any moment." I turned back around and stared through the window. Levi moved closer and stood next to me.

"Yeah, looks awful in there. Everyone's laughing, drinking beer." I looked at him out of the corner of my eye. "Horrific, really." His lips curved into a small smile.

"Smartass," I said with a grin.

"Want to go grab a coffee?" Levi shoved his hands into his pockets. It was a harmless question, but my mind wandered to the first date that Parker and I had together. When things were different, simple.

"I'm taking you on a proper date tomorrow," Parker said.

I sat on my bed and curled my legs underneath me. I tried to contain my excitement as Parker talked about us going to the movies and dinner. Other than the English class I was a teacher's aide in, that's the only time we ever got to see each other. It wasn't enough.

Not anymore.

"Have you written any more? There's a big assignment due in your English class on Monday."

Parker laughed. "I'll do it Monday the period before. That's how I roll."

I scoffed.

"You disapprove?"

"I don't know how you do it. My anxiety would be sky-high if I started the weekend without all of my homework done." I lay back on my bed and stared up at the ceiling.

"You need to live, Rainey. You're a teenager, not a nun." He sighed. "We only get one life. Don't waste it."

"Look at you getting all philosophical on me." I giggled. "But you're right. I'd love to live a bit more. Whatever that means."

"Where's your mom?" Parker asked.

"Working the overnight shift. Just me, myself, and I tonight."

"Great. I'm coming over. No work today. Sleepover. I'll bring snacks."

I jumped up out of bed. "Wait, what?" I stared at myself in the mirror, my hair was a mess at the top of my head staring back at me, along with my splotchy face and the ever-cool retainer that lined my pearly whites.

"Living starts now. See you in about an hour." Parker hung up the phone, and I stared in awe at the

phone screen. He was coming over. Parker was on his way to my house for a sleepover. Instead of getting myself more presentable, I dialed Ava.

"Hey!" she answered. "What's up?"

"Parker's on his way over, and I'm freaking out!" I ripped open a drawer and rummaged through it to find a better set of pajamas or something.

"Holy shit, and your mom isn't home? Bow Chicka Wow Wow."

"Oh God. Do you think he's expecting sex? I'm not ready for that. We haven't even gone out on a date yet." I groaned as I held up a T-shirt that said y+u=us from my boy band loving days.

"He's Parker. Not ever sure what he's thinking," Ava said. "Girl, get to know him. Have fun. Relax."

"But my mom. I should ask her first."

Ava laughed. "Your mom's cool, but she won't be home until morning. She doesn't have to know. And plus, if she said no, would you turn him away at your door? The tall, dark, and handsome boy who was your fantasy all summer?"

"Well, no." Ava did have a point.

"There. So, it doesn't matter what your mom says. I know you like to play by the rules, but tonight, try something different—and send me pictures!" I giggled. Butterflies fluttered in my stomach.

"Okay. I have to go find something other than my boy band T-shirts to wear."

"Good luck with that. Don't do anything I'd do!"

Ava hung up, and I was left with my overflowing drawers and anticipation that was going to kill me.

***

I jumped when I heard the first creak of the stairs that led up to my fifth-floor apartment. It was a pain traveling up those stairs with loads of groceries, but it was ours. A place that my mother and I both worked hard to keep. I didn't pay bills. My mother believed firmly that it was her job to take care of me, but I helped clean and attempted to cook as often as I could. School work and my part-time job kept me occupied. I liked to stay busy and have goals to strive for. I opened the door to the hallway before Parker even made it to the top. I knew it looked overeager, but the truth was, I was terrified. Looking down at my pink flowy top and yoga pants, I swear I expected to see my knees knocking together.

"Hey." Looking up, I fought back a giggle at the sight of him. He wore a ratty T-shirt and plaid pajama bottoms that looked a little too small. They were high waters and showed the white of his socks. "Like my outfit?" He spun around.

A giggle escaped my lips. "I would have kept on my band T-shirt had I known this is how you were coming over." I opened the door and motioned him inside.

"Depends. What band?" He quirked up his left eyebrow.

"Maroon 5. I never got to see them in concert, but Ava did and bought me a shirt."

"Nice. Where should I put these?" Parker held up his hands, the two shopping bags overflowing. "I wasn't sure what you liked, so I got a bit of every snack food there was. I have chips, chocolate, fruit just in case you want an apple instead of peanut M & M's for some unknown reason...." I watched him empty the contents of the bag on the coffee table, how he put the candy in one pile, the chips in another. Everything about him seemed so carefree, yet there were parts that were structured, organized, thoughtful.

"What? Do I have a booger in my nose?" He flared his nostrils in the most ungodly way that allowed me to see straight up his nose.

"Ew, that's nasty. No booger." I snickered.

"Ah. I'm handsome, right? It's the plaid high waters." He stretched out his long leg, further hiking up the pants. "I knew they'd make you fall for me. My devilish plan succeeded!"

Fall for him? My mind raced with hope, possibility, and straight-up lust. It was a mishmash of emotions. I didn't know whether to tell him I had fallen for him in an I-want-to-lick-your-face-off sort of way since that day in the diner or to tell him that I hoped we could maybe explore something more between us. My mind, ever so active as it was, frantically searched for a response as he stared at me, a Snickers bar in one hand and a bag of Doritos in the other.

"You're all right," I squeaked out. Smooth. Real smooth. After toying with what to say, that's what I came up with? Ava would have a fit.

"All right? Damn, way to make a man grow a complex." With a frown, he threw the Snickers and Doritos on the table.

"Oh, I didn't mean just all right. I didn't want to sound too eager. Like damn, Parker, I've thought about you since I first saw you at the diner. Or that I love the way you're honest and kind without being fake. And how you're not just all right, you're the most superbly handsome man I've ever met." I took a breath and felt my cheeks heat. Well, I'd done it again. Spouted off more than necessary. I'd turned to walk into the kitchen to compose and probably scold myself when Parker grabbed my arm and spun me around to face him.

"Don't run. Stay." His words caressed my body and enveloped me in warmth. The insecurity was still there, but more subtle, masked with the comfort that his hand on me brought.

"I didn't mean to say all that. I'm sorry if I made you uncomfortable."

He released my arm and sighed. "The only thing that's made me uncomfortable these past weeks is wanting to be with you and not knowing whether to just say it." Parker smiled at me. "But I think you feel something, even if a small piece of you. It's drawn to me. Isn't it?"

I opened my mouth, but nothing came out. He wants to be with me? *I nodded.*

"Let's stop pretending that we aren't interested romantically in each other. I'm not seeing anyone else or interested in dating anyone else, are you?"

"Not at all. I haven't dated in forever." I mentally smacked myself. Way to make yourself look cool, Rainey.

"So, what do you say we call this what it is, a date. Our first official date as boyfriend and girlfriend." Parker held out his hand to me, and I wanted nothing more than to jump up and down.

I placed my hand in his; it fit perfectly.

We sat down on my couch, and he kept his hand in mine. Our fingers intertwined and some nonsense show that kept him laughing played in the background. Nothing could make this night more special.

"Rainey?" Levi's voice brought me back to the present. "Are you okay?" I brushed a tear that streamed down my face.

"I'm not. I'm so sorry. I can't have coffee right now. I can't do this right now." I flung up my hands, motioning toward the bar where all my coworkers were hanging out. "I'm not ready." I rushed back to my car without as much as a goodbye to Levi. There was nothing wrong with him. His intentions were pure, but me? I was hurting. Damaged goods.

Finally making it to my car, I pulled out my cell phone and called Ava.

"Hey, my sister from another mister," Ava answered.

"My marriage is over. I'm getting a divorce. How is this my life, Ava?" I propped my head on the steering wheel and cried.

"Oh, sweetie. No one plans for this to happen when they get married, but you'll be better for it. I promise. There are so many amazing things in your future. I can feel it."

"I'm glad you can feel it, because right now I feel like I'm breaking into tiny pieces. I know he cheated. I know that this is for the best, but why does it hurt so bad?" I wiped my eyes on my shirt.

"Because you've been together your entire lives. You guys were high school sweethearts, and you're starting over, and that can be scary." She paused. "Listen to me, Rainey, you're strong. You don't give yourself enough credit sometimes for all the amazing things that you've accomplished in your life. Stop selling yourself short. Pick up those broken pieces and put them back together. It might look a little different, but that's the point. Not everything is going to be the same, but that's the beauty of life. Even when it seems like we can't go on any longer, something exciting happens and we push on and become a better version of ourselves."

"Since when do you speak like that?" I laughed. Ava was always there for me, but her words were usually more about getting off my ass. Not quite so poetic.

"I may have read some inspirational shit on the

Internet to help you out. Now, enough of that. Go back to the bar, have a drink or two, and try to have a good time." There's my best friend.

After we said our goodbyes, I walked back to the bar and headed straight inside. Everyone greeted me with open arms. I looked around for Levi, wanting to apologize for running off when he asked me to go grab coffee, but he was nowhere to be found.

"Here. Have a beer!" Jean shoved a beer into my hand.

"Thanks!" I yelled over the music.

I nursed the same beer all night. I had a good time just being out of the house and attempting to bring myself closer to who I was before, although I had no idea who that was anymore. One piece was firmly put back in place. Only a few more to go.

CHAPTER EIGHT

I opened the door to our crummy apartment after another long day. I'd been in class since the morning, then headed straight to the diner to work the late shift. I was pretty sure my eyes were bloodshot, and my legs were going to give out at any moment.

As I opened the apartment door, the darkness greeted me. I hated when Parker turned off all the lights. Who the hell knew what was lurking in the shadows? At least that's what I thought all the time. I was a wimp. I placed my backpack on the couch, but not before turning on every light I could.

"Jesus!" I jumped back, seeing Parker sitting on the couch with the biggest grin on his face.

"Hello," he said as he held out a dozen lilies. Lilies were my favorite, the white so pure and beautiful. Perfectly flawless.

"What's all of this for?" I leaned over and placed a

kiss to his lips.

"I think it's time I made an honest woman out of you."

I stumbled back into the chair. "What?" I croaked out.

Parker placed the flowers on the secondhand coffee table that someone gave us when we got this apartment. He walked over to me and got down on one knee and pulled out a simple gold band with a heart on it. It wasn't fancy, expensive, or anything that you'd see in a bridal magazine, but my God did it take my breath away. It was mine.

"I've known since the first day I saw you at the diner that you were something special. The thought of not coming home to you every day for the rest of my life isn't something I want to even imagine. Marry me, Rainey, please?"

All I could do was shake my head yes as he slipped the ring on my finger.

"My mother's going to kill me," I whispered against his lips.

"It's okay, we'll always have each other. We'll tell her together."

I woke up in a cold sweat, my hair clinging to my face and my clothes to my body. We never did tell my mom, not until a week later, after we went off and got married at the Justice of the Peace. She wasn't happy; she said we were too young and a lot could change. But we were young and in love, and that was enough for us.

I guess sometimes love wasn't enough.

My phone buzzed on my nightstand, and I groaned, noticing the number for the hospital. It was my day off. I wondered who the hell called out.

"All right, who called out?" I answered the phone.

"Rainey, Emily, Parker's sister, was just brought in for an overdose. Parker's her emergency contact, but with him being gone... I'm sorry, I wasn't sure what to do." Melissa, the ER receptionist, said, her voice shaking.

I jumped out of bed and threw on sweatpants and a T-shirt while trying to balance my phone. "No. No. You did the right thing. I'm on my way."

I rushed out of the house without so much as brushing my teeth. I managed to send a quick email to Parker, and hoped he got it. Although we were divorcing, I wasn't going to let his sister, someone I had grown to love and care about, sit in the hospital alone. She was family. She always would be.

I made it to the hospital in record time, rushing into the ER.

"What happened?" I asked Lucy, one of the nurses who was sitting behind the desk.

"She came in seizing out of control and foaming at the mouth. The paramedic saved her life by giving her Narcan. Thank God he had it, or we would have been making a different call." Lucy brought me in for a hug. "She's in room 202. She needs help, that's for sure. You should see her arms. Covered in track marks." I nodded as I put my hair in a ponytail on the top of my head. Emily had needed help for a long time, but like Parker she refused it. That was one of the few things they had in common, their stubbornness.

I headed to her room and slowly opened the door, focusing on the equipment sounds. It was something that I was accustomed to from the years working in the hospital, but this was different. I loved Emily, even though she had her own issues. She was kind, loving, and had such a good heart. I'd tried to set her on the straight and narrow, but her childhood damaged her much worse than it did Parker. I guess they both were damaged in different ways. Parker ran to war and sought solace in the chaos. Emily sought comfort in sex and drugs and ended up a pregnant teen that resulted in her giving her baby up for adoption. It's funny how two people from the exact same environment could turn out completely different.

I checked all her machines to make sure everything was working properly and pulled the chair next to her. Taking her hand in mine, I spoke out loud.

"Oh, Emily, what have you done?" I looked over her scarred arms, the track marks marring her beautiful alabaster skin. Emily was beautiful, with her long blonde hair and stunning blue eyes. She was tall and thin and could have easily been a model if she didn't take a different path in life. She could have been so many things.

I rubbed her hand and spoke about the latest news.

I even pulled out my phone and read some of the latest Hollywood gossip that she always seemed to love. I stepped out when my phone rang, noticing it was a private number.

"Hey, Rainey. Is Emily okay?" I swallowed hard at the sound of Parker's voice. I hadn't spoken to him since he told me he had found someone else. No messages or calls. Although, I had typed and deleted many angry emails. Hearing his voice was like reopening a wound, and I flinched.

"She's okay for now. Stable, but she needs help." I paced up and down the hallway.

"I know. I'm trying to get emergency leave. I hate to ask this, but any chance you can make sure the doctors send over documentation to the Red Cross? They won't grant me the leave unless they have it. I need to be there to help set her up in rehab once and for all."

He was coming home? The thought of seeing him made butterflies form in my stomach. I wasn't ready to see him. Not now, not after everything. I took a breath to bring myself back to reality. This wasn't about him and me. This was about Emily. His only sister.

"Of course. I'll take care of it. Let me know when you know that you'll be home, and I can get you at the airport."

Oh sure. Just offer to do something else from him. That makes sense.

"Thanks, Rainey. I appreciate you being there for her."

"She's like my sister too. I've known her a long time."

"Yeah" was all he managed to get out.

I glanced up as Dr. Rodgers waved as he exited her room. "The doctor just saw her, so I'm going to go and get some information. I'll keep you informed via email."

"Sounds good. Thanks again, Rainey. I love—" His words halted as he cleared his throat. Saying I love you was like second nature to us both.

"Goodbye, Parker."

Clutching the phone in my hand, I took a breath.

"Hey, I'm sorry to hear about your sister-in-law." Dr. Rodgers came over and placed his hand on my shoulder and squeezed.

"Thanks. What's the verdict?" I placed my phone into my pocket, trying to switch focus onto what he was going to say.

"She OD'ed on heroin. Looks like it was a bad batch. She needs rehab like yesterday. I have a few places I can recommend and pull some strings at any of them for you. A lot of them have a long waiting list."

"Thanks. I appreciate that."

"Of course." His name was called over the intercom, and he headed off.

And there I was, left in the middle of the hallway, not knowing what the hell to do next. I put my face in my heads and let out a small, muffled scream.

"Rainey?" I lifted my head just as Levi came into view.

"Hi." I pulled down my ratty T-shirt and patted my hair. I was a mess.

"What brings you here on your day off?" He tried to keep his eyes on mine, but they kept shifting to my body. I knew I looked like shit.

"My sister-in-law was brought in for an OD. Hence the lovely outfit and rat's nest of a hairdo." I motioned to my hair.

He folded his arms across his chest. "The young girl? I was the paramedic on scene. How's she doing?"

Of course he was the paramedic on scene.

"She's stable. That's the best we can ask for right now." I tapped my foot on the ground, my nervousness making me fidget. I didn't know why just being around Levi was making me so antsy. Was I attracted to him? Sure. But I was currently dealing with my soon-to-be ex-husband's sister and knee-deep in depression. I was pretty sure I wasn't thinking straight.

"About the other night too, I'm sorry for running you off after you asked me to have coffee. I've been slightly emotional lately."

That's an understatement. I leaned up against the wall, feeling a bit better since I'd apologized.

"Want to go grab a coffee now? The cafeteria has shitty food and coffee, but you can make it up to me and tell me all about the spot you're in. I've been told I'm a good listener." He smiled, and I shivered, pulling my arms around myself. Coffee. That's all he was asking of me. I wasn't prepared for much else, even if he looked handsome in his uniform.

"Don't you have to work?" I pushed off the wall and gave him the sassiest look I could.

"We do get breaks." He laughed, showing his perfect white teeth. *Did he have a flaw?*

"Okay. Coffee sounds good. If you can stand being seen with a walking zombie. I didn't even brush my teeth."

Levi started laughing. He fished around in his pocket and tossed me a piece of gum. "I think the zombie look suits you. But I draw the line at stinky breath." He winked.

"Why thank you, kind sir." We walked quietly to the cafeteria, and for the first time in a while, the depression and the fact that my life was falling apart wasn't weighing on me. I could handle this, and I would come out stronger. Tougher. Even if I had to claw my way out.

CHAPTER NINE

Levi and I sat drinking coffee in the poorly lit cafeteria. He didn't push me with questions about why I left him hanging for coffee the first time; instead, we asked each other mindless questions. It was fun and made me feel like a kid again.

"Favorite color?" he asked, sipping on his coffee.

"Green," I said, with a smile. "It reminds me of everything. The grass. Life." Levi blinked excessively. "What? Too much, right? I have a tendency to be a bit too dramatic," I confessed.

"No. That's my favorite too. Seems we have a bit in common." He looked up at the ceiling and smiled. "I've got a good one. Stars Wars or Star Trek?"

"Star Wars all the way. I used to dress like Princess Leia when I was younger." I tapped my fingers on the table.

"You're up. I've asked the past couple."

"Well, obviously you like coffee." I held up my cup in celebration.

"Erh." He averted his eyes. "I have a confession."

I gasped and brought my hand to my heart. "Don't say it. Don't you dare."

"I hate coffee. I drink tea." He hung his head in shame.

I placed my coffee gently on the table. "That's it. We can't be friends."

"I tried. I really did. You had me at Star Wars, but if coffee is the deciding factor, I can understand that." He acted like he was getting ready to get up.

I looked over at Levi. I barely knew him, other than the few times we'd crossed paths and laughed together. But the questions, the conversation flowed effortlessly. I needed this. A friend other than Ava who I could just chat with. He brought me comfort and a sliver of happiness.

"So, my marriage is over. Parker's been cheating on me for God knows how long."

Levi gently put down his cup of tea, his eyes softening. "Damn, Raindrop, I'm sorry. I know what that's like. Especially after you put so much into it."

"Yeah." I brushed away a tear that had fallen. "We're still so connected. His sister is like my sister. I care. It sucks. I wish I could walk away from it all, but here I am taking care of his sister." I threw up my hands. "Hell, I'm waiting to find out when he'll be flying in on emergency leave so I can pick him up and carve the wound open that is my heart even more."

Levi sat back in his chair, making himself more comfortable. Stretching out his legs in front of him, he played with his beard. "That says a lot about you, that you can't just walk away. You guys were together since you were teenagers. It also says a lot about you as a person. You're caring. Kind. Genuine."

I scoffed. "I'm weak."

"Why do you think that?" Levi raised an eyebrow.

"You want to know my first thought when he told me he found someone else?" Levi nodded. "What did she have that I didn't? Why was he willing to put in the effort with someone new but not with me? I'm not enough. I never have been."

Levi shot forward and took my hand in his. "Bullshit. I know enough about you from what I've seen that you're all those things I mentioned and then some. You deserve happiness, and someday you'll realize what a package you are."

I slowly pulled my hand from his, relishing the feeling that lingered. It was comfort, reassurance, everything I needed.

"Thanks, Levi." I dabbed my eyes with the napkin. "So those are my issues. I'm insecure and about to be divorced at twenty-six. Amazing, huh?"

Levi took a sip of his tea. "Here." He pulled out his phone and slid it to me. "Put in your number."

"What?" I looked at his phone like it was a dead

mouse. Had I not scared him away with my self-pity?

"You need a friend. Someone to pull you off your ass and make you realize there is an entire life ahead of you worth living." Funny, Parker had been that for me once.

I typed in my number. "You remind me of my best friend, Ava. She tells me to get off my ass all the time."

"Good. I like her already." The way he smiled made me uneasy. It brought about feelings that I hadn't experienced in a while. Excitement. Endless possibilities.

I stretched and looked at the clock on my phone. "I'm sure your break is almost over, and I should be getting back to Emily so I can be there when she wakes up."

"Right. Yeah." Levi and I then stood awkwardly. I couldn't explain it, that feeling when there's just a connection with someone. That's how it felt when he was around, like a low buzz was constantly in the air.

I gave him a sideways hug. "It was nice talking with you. Thank you for listening to me."

"You too. Text you soon so we can get your ass off the couch."

"Sounds good." I walked away, not without glancing back and grinning as he tried to play it off that he wasn't looking at my ass. I was in horrible sweatpants, but the fact that he still tried to look flattered me.

I knew I wasn't ready for anything romantic with

anyone, but Levi might just be good for my healing. Everyone needed good friends in their lives, and Levi was proving to be just what I needed.

CHAPTER TEN

I wanted nothing more than to chuck my laptop across the room. There Parker was, with a new profile picture with his new girl. We hadn't even officially filed for a divorce, and he was making it known that I was out of the picture. She was gorgeous, with her long blondish hair and stunning green eyes. She had the perfect figure, and the smiles on their faces damn near killed me. They were happy. I was miserable.

They both were in uniform and clearly not supposed to be taking selfies. I wanted nothing more than to forward the picture to their commanding officer and say, "Fraternizing much?" but that wasn't my style, even though sometimes I wished it was.

I spent the next hour Facebook stalking her. I knew where she'd gone to high school, how many brothers and sisters she had. I leaned back against my couch when I found myself on her parents' Facebook page.

I officially had become a crazy woman. I hated her. I hated him. Why couldn't that be me? I didn't even want to say her name, *Samantha*.

"Why am I torturing myself?" I clicked the laptop shut, trying to put Parker and Samantha out of sight and out of mind. Padding into the kitchen, I cringed at my reflection in the refrigerator. My pants were a little tighter than normal; all the ice cream and chocolate I'd been eating had gone straight to my waist. That didn't stop me though. I opened the freezer to grab another carton; this time Cherry Garcia called my name.

This was what depression was for me, eating my weight in candy and anything that I could easily shove into my mouth. What did it matter anymore? Gone were my days of running and caring about what I looked like. I'd never be enough. I wasn't enough for Parker. I wasn't enough for anyone, especially myself.

My cell phone buzzed, and I placed the ice cream on the counter. I recognized the few messages Levi and I had exchanged over the week.

Levi: What are you doing?

Me: About to eat my weight in ice cream, you?

Levi: That sounds interesting. I just got up. About to go to the beach. Want to join?

The beach? I wasn't particularly fond of the beach. I liked the sand, and I loved to swim, but there were things in the ocean. Like sharks. Or jellyfish.

But I had no plans. I never had any plans except for when Ava came around. I looked over at the carton of ice cream that was on the counter. Somehow that ice cream became symbolic for everything in my life. If I placed another spoonful in my mouth, I was letting Parker win. Letting him get under my skin and control me like he had these past years.

Leaving the ice cream on the counter, I texted Levi back.

Me: Sounds good. My address is 146 Highland Street. I'll be ready in a few.

There was no way a few minutes was enough time. I tried to find something to wear that would look halfway decent on me. I wasn't a typical beach-going type, so my bathing suit selection was scarce. I settled on a black one-piece that hid enough of my ice cream indiscretions and had some tummy-slimming device that made me want to kiss whoever invented it.

Throwing on a yellow sundress over the bathing suit, I grabbed my sunglasses and slipped on my flip-flops just as my doorbell rang.

"Heya, Raindrop." Levi stood propped against my doorframe. He always wore simple T-shirts. I liked simple. Simple was refreshing for a change. This one was plain orange and matched the swim shorts that hung loosely around his hips. "You look pretty. Yellow suits you."

"Thanks." I blushed. "Ready?" I picked up my bag that I had packed with a few things I'd need for the beach and latched the door behind me.

I was nervous. I'd grown so accustomed to Parker

and knew everything about him. What he liked, what he didn't like. I knew how far I could push my sarcastic sense of humor without going too far—I just knew. I thought of all the times we did outings like this together, and I could count on my hand how many times we went out. He preferred to stay in, which meant I preferred to stay in. He never knew much about me, now that I thought about it. I'd invested myself into ensuring I knew my husband inside and out; he invested himself in other things.

Parker: I ordered pizza for dinner. I'll bring it home with me.

I smiled at Parker's text message, relieved that I didn't have to worry about dinner tonight after working all day at the diner and then going to my clinical.

I got home and got comfortable, waiting for Parker to come home with dinner. I prepared the TV with our favorite shows and sipped on my glass of wine.

"Hey." Parker came into the house, the smell of pizza wafting in the air.

"That smells so good!" I jumped up and pulled down some plates. Parker padded into the bedroom to change out of his uniform.

Opening the pizza, I frowned. Pepperoni. I hated pepperoni.

"What?" Parker looked over at me as he plated himself a few slices.

"I hate pepperoni." I peeled it off the slice I chose, cheese and sauce coming with it.

"How the hell am I supposed to know that?" Parker shrugged. I brushed aside the ache in my chest at his words. I knew he loved combination pizza the best and thought pineapple on pizza was an atrocity to all pizza lovers everywhere. He hated peas with a passion and used to hide them in his milk when he was younger. I knew his favorite beer. I knew everything because I cared and wanted him to be happy.

Taking my seminaked pizza, I curled up next to Parker and brushed aside my emotions. Someday he'd remember I hated pepperoni. For now, I'd just take care of everything.

"I hate pepperoni on pizza," I blurted out.

Smooth, Rainey. Smooth.

Levi laughed. "Noted." He tapped his temple. "Steel vault here. I'll never forget that nugget of information."

I smiled politely as he opened his car door. He'd forget, but it didn't matter. I always had my Ben and Jerry's to keep me company. They'd never let me down.

***

I slathered on another layer of sunblock, my skin sizzling. It was fucking hot. I was pretty sure I could fry an egg on my skin right then.

"Come on! Cool off." Levi pulled me off the towel, and I groaned.

"There's stuff in the ocean." I cringed, thinking of all the slimy things that could potentially brush against me. Or eat me.

He laughed, and it traveled all the way down to my toes. He had that way about him. A carefree life that made me want to join him. "That there is," he said.

I squinted so I could see him better. "How are you not cooking in the sun? You're paler than me. Vampireish, really." I poked his arm.

"Hate to break it you, but I'm not a vampire."

I snapped my fingers. "Shucks. I love to watch a man sparkle in the sun."

"Otherwise I'd suck your blood. We wouldn't want that, would we?" He leaned in closer, his words kissing my ears.

Levi's eyes lingered over my neck, and my hand instinctively massaged the area. Like him sucking my neck would be a bad thing.

Here. Bleed me dry.

"Race you!" I took off in a sprint, not caring if any of my parts were jiggling, and dived into the ocean. It was refreshing against my heated skin, and for a brief second, I forgot all about the stuff that was floating around in the ocean.

Lying on my back, I closed my eyes and floated. I heard Levi's voice, but it was muffled, as most of my head was in the water. I placed my feet down to stand and felt something slimy—and I swore there were teeth, possibly even fangs that brushed against my thigh.

"Oh. My. God. Something has me!" I jumped into

Levi's arms. He caught me effortlessly and chuckled.

"What's so funny? There's something down there. Is it a shark? A flesh-eating fish?" Levi pulled me closer and dipped his hand down into the water, pulling out a fistful of seaweed.

"Here's the culprit. I don't see any deadly teeth, but why don't you get a closer look." He dangled the seaweed over my stomach as I clung to him for dear life.

"Stop!" I screeched with laughter.

Discarding the seaweed back into the ocean, Levi looked down at me, his blue eyes accentuated by the sun.

"I refuse to touch the bottom," I whispered, trying to shift gears back to the killer seaweed and not how delicious he looked in the sun.

With a bit of maneuvering, he positioned me on his back. I resisted the urge to lick it, mostly because it was covered in ocean water and would be salty. Levi wasn't overly built, but toned in all the right places. I was a sucker for a nice back.

"Here, wrap your legs around me." I did as he said and found myself being carted around on Levi's back, enjoying the ocean, minus the creepy-crawlies that lurked beneath.

"Is this good?" he asked as he waded out deeper into the water.

Resting my head against his back, I smiled. "It's perfect." And it was. Way better than Ben and Jerry's and yelling at romance movies on TV.

***

"I had a good time." I played with the ends of my hair, trying to avoid eye contact with Levi. I really did have a good time, much more than I expected I would. Something had changed though. A shift in how we looked at each other. That chemistry was always there, now that I thought about it, from the first day that we met and I yelled at him. Now, it was more pronounced and much harder to ignore.

"I did too. I'm glad we got to hang out." My heart rate quickened. Out of the corner of my eye, I watched him lick his lips. I could almost taste them against mine, but I wasn't ready for that. Not yet. It wasn't for a lack of attraction, but I didn't want to go from one relationship to the next, to use Levi as a means to forget how badly Parker had hurt me. There was still a lot of closure needed with Parker as well. It wouldn't have been fair to either of us. Right? But my God, did I want to kiss him, to just have something for myself for once.

"I can't kiss you, Levi," I blurted out, turning toward him. I expected Levi to look at me like I was stupid, but he didn't; he laughed softly before gently stroking my cheek.

"I know, Raindrop."

I opened my eyes that I hadn't even realized I closed.

"Goodbye," I said as I opened the car door.

"Have a good night."

I stood on the sidewalk and waved as he drove away.

Once inside my house, I showered and changed into my pajamas. I didn't turn on sappy romance movies or hide under my blanket. I watched a comedy and didn't once think about the melting Ben and Jerry's that had been sitting on my counter since this morning.

CHAPTER ELEVEN

I never got sick, but of course on Senior Day I was holed up in my house fighting off the flu. I could barely get up to use the bathroom, let alone shower. If my nostrils weren't clogged and I didn't sound like a congested pig, I was sure what I smelled like wouldn't be pleasant.

A knock at my door made me groan, and I stumbled out of bed. In my oversized nightshirt and fluffy bunny slippers, I opened the door, blowing my nose.

"Parker?" I sneezed, my hair, which was on the top of my head, escaping from the hair tie and falling not so gracefully around my face.

"I brought you soup and flowers." He stepped forward and placed a kiss on my forehead. "Jesus, you're burning up. Come on, I'll take care of you."

"No!" I held up my hand and backed away. "I'm contagious."

Parker smiled and closed the door behind him. "I don't care. I'm going to give you some medicine and let you curl up against me while we watch TV. I'm freezing. We can put that heat to good use."

I looked at the window and noticed his car wasn't parked outside.

"Where's your car?"

"It needs a new battery. I walked." He moved around my apartment like he lived there. He pretty much did now. My mom had grown fond of him, and since he lived on friends' couches versus living with his abusive parents, he was here a lot.

"That's like seven miles!" I screeched.

Turning toward me, he handed me a few pills. "You were worth every one of those miles."

Maybe it was the fever and I was delirious, but I was going to marry this boy. We were going to have babies and be madly in love, because he was perfect and I loved him.

***

Parker was able to get emergency leave, but with travel time and everything, he wouldn't be home until the end of the week. That left me to ensure Emily was adjusting to her rehab facility okay. I didn't mind lending a hand. Emily wasn't aware of what was going on with her brother and me, and with all that was going on with her, she didn't need that on her mind right now.

She needed to focus on getting better.

I wasn't sharing my and Parker's business with everyone. It wasn't that I was hiding it; it just wasn't the best conversation starter. "Hey so, I'm getting a divorce. Do you want to go grab burgers?" Plus, although I knew it was the best thing for us both, I was still trying to adjust. Although now that he'd posted a new picture on Facebook, I was sure I'd have to do some explaining sooner rather than later.

Walking into the rehab facility, I checked in at the nurses' station and walked down the long, narrow hallway. I never paid much attention to hospitals. Everything was sterile and white; there was no color, no vibrancy. The ER was much different. I suppose the hustle and bustle distracted me enough that I didn't pay much attention to the ambiance. I didn't understand how this could be seen as a healing environment. To me, healing was all about exposing yourself to life, stepping outside of what had been comfortable your entire life and just living. Like the beach and creepy sea creatures.

I headed to the group room where visitation was allowed. The door was propped open, and the sound of people talking traveled into the hallway. Once I rounded the corner, I saw Emily. She sat in a chair in front of a wooden table that looked worse for wear. Scratches lined the surface, and all the chairs looked like they'd buckle at any moment. A puzzle was in front of her, partially done. She clutched a puzzle piece in her hand and something else in the other, and stared down, seemingly lost in thought. The chair squeaked as she turned to face me, bringing what was in her other hand to my sight. It was a printed email. Tears streamed down her face as her eyes bored into me.

"What's wrong?" I said quietly as I pulled a chair next to her. The few other families that were in the room were focused on each other, for which I was grateful. I wanted as much privacy with Emily as possible.

"Parker wrote me an email, and the nurse printed it out for me." She fisted the paper tighter, turning it into a ball. I didn't say anything to coax her into telling me more, I waited. "You can imagine I was surprised when he mentioned you guys divorcing and how he met someone else. When were you going to tell me, Rainey?" Her words were cold as ice. *Fuck.* I didn't want her to feel like I was keeping something from her. I was just trying to protect her, keep her mind focused on her rehab and not Parker and me. I reached out to take her hand in mine, but she snatched it away.

"It's complicated," I said with a sigh. I hadn't wanted her to find out like this. "I wanted you to focus on you. Not on your brother and me."

Placing the balled-up paper on the table, she turned to face me. Her eyes were bloodshot, her face a ghastly shade of gray.

"You and my brother were the last hope that I had in this fucked-up world." She let out a breathy laugh. "I thought that with you two, and all that you've been through and accomplished together, that love conquered all. Guess I was wrong."

I felt tears pressing against my eyes and pushed back my emotions. I wanted to let it all out, to tell Emily that I felt what she did and was so incredibly confused, but I couldn't. I had to be her reassurance even when the idea of love, the forever kind, seemed like a load of shit right now.

"Why can't you guys just make it work? This isn't like returning a shirt you don't like. This is your marriage." Emily's voice rose, and people started staring.

"Sometimes people just grow apart. We're both so different. Even when we met in high school, that was glaringly obvious. The distance kept things exciting, and when things got choppy, Parker would leave again, and the honeymoon stage would start again, but the honeymoon stage isn't enough for either of us anymore. He's married to the army, and that's okay. That's what he loves. That's what he's good at."

"He said he loved you in the email. That he always will."

Of course he did. He could never say that stuff to me.

"And I will always love him. Your brother was my first love. Something like that doesn't just go away." Even though I wanted it all to. The young love that Parker and I had was so painful. It was a part of my identity. It grew with me. It became a part of me and made me lose parts of myself.

Emily picked at her fingernails, drawing blood from her thumb. "What about us? Where does that leave us?" She let out a whimper. "Everyone leaves. My mother left. My dad left. Parker leaves. I'll be more alone now than ever. Drugs numb all that." If my heart wasn't already broken, it would have shattered into pieces. She didn't deserve the shitty cards life had dealt her. No one did. But hearing that she turned to drugs to try to make it all disappear was difficult.

Bringing Emily in for a hug, I whispered against her shoulder, "I'll never leave you. You've become my sister just as much as you're Parker's. I'll always be here for you."

Emily pulled away and stood up, the legs of the chair scraping against the floor.

"Everyone leaves. That's reality." Standing in the doorway, she added, "I'll stick with what I can count on."

I stayed at the table, finishing the puzzle and getting lost in my own thoughts. I wanted so badly to be there for Emily, and I would be, but something she said stuck with me. Everyone leaves. Nothing lasts, no matter how hard you try, and I was living proof of that.

CHAPTER TWELVE

Nothing could prepare you for picking up your soon-to-be ex-husband at the airport after not seeing him for months. I knew I should have let him take a taxi, or walk for that matter, but that wasn't me. God, why couldn't that be me? I was always nervous when I saw Parker after a long time away, but this was different. The anxiousness and dread in my stomach made me want to vomit. There was a part of me that would love Parker forever. We had been through so much together that I knew those feelings wouldn't just wash away. A part of us would always be connected. Maybe we'd be friends. Maybe someday it wouldn't hurt so much, but right now, the pain was poignant.

Parker came down the escalator, his assault pack on his back, accentuating his muscles. He always bulked up more during deployments, spending all his free time in the gym. His usually pale skin had a tan with a hint of redness. My eyes followed him all the way down, and I couldn't help the smile that flitted across my face. I remembered one of our homecomings and how excited I was to see him.

I swore my heart was going to beat out of my chest. I never imagined loving someone could feel like this, that I could feel both anxious and excited at the same time. I'd waited a year to see my husband. When we eloped, no one supported us, no one believed in us, but we would make it. I knew we would.

People started cheering; the sounds of voices thanking soldiers for their service traveled through the airport. I pulled down my dress, cursing myself for choosing one that was a little more revealing. After a year apart, I wanted to look my best.

Parker rounded the corner, and despite everyone being dressed exactly the same, I could pick him out of a sea of soldiers. He was tall, his chiseled features distinct from everyone else's. Then his eyes found mine and locked on me. The sparkle and desire I saw made my knees buckle, and before I could blink, he dropped his bag and we ran toward each other.

The embrace was even better than any Hollywood movie. My legs wrapped around his waist, and he held me up with a satisfied grunt.

"You look beautiful, Rainey. I missed you so much." I couldn't find the words to tell him how much I missed him, or how hard this year had been; instead, our lips met and our clashing tongues did all

the talking that I couldn't.

My husband was home. We were whole again.

It was a good memory, one of my favorites of Parker and me. He didn't drop his bag this time, his eyes didn't sparkle or linger over my body. They were filled with regret, loss, even confusion. I offered a small smile, which he returned, albeit reluctantly. Gone was the passion and love. All we had were our memories.

"Hey," Parker said, shuffling his bag between his shoulders. "Thanks for picking me up. I appreciate it."

"Of course." I smiled wide, trying not to show my sadness. If I could fake it enough, maybe I would believe it.

"Are you okay?" Parker stared at me, squinting. That was the thing about being married for so long, there wasn't much I could get past him.

"Yeah. It's just hard to see you. After everything."

He nodded. "Let's go home." He snapped his mouth shut, realizing what he'd said. It was home once, but now it was just another place. Another memory.

"We're going to have to work together this next week. Emily needs us. The focus should be on her, okay?" I said the words out loud, but they were more for me, to remind myself of the mission at hand. Emily. Her drug addiction. Not Parker and me.

"Roger that." Parker grinned and took the keys from my hand. "I'm driving."

I led the way to the car and stole glances of Parker. We were both so different now. He was hardened from his times at war, the poetry that used to seep from his gorgeous lips now replaced with curse words, regret, and hate. I'd forever hold on to those poems, the words that made me fall in love with him. Because that reality was much better than the stranger that stood before me.

✳✳✳

We drove home in silence. It wasn't awkward, but we both were just lost in our minds. I was anxious to see how things were going to go once we were under the roof that we shared for many years, the place that he came home to after countless deployments.

I helped Parker carry in his bags and thought of all the places we made love, and the mornings I'd burn breakfast and Parker would smile and eat the scorched toast and tell me how great it was. That didn't last long, but I held on to it, something that kept me attached to a marriage that had ended years ago.

We went to our separate areas of the house. I caught Parker grabbing boxes and starting to pack up some of his belongings. I didn't know where he was going to go. I honestly didn't want to know, because I was sure it would be to her. Where they could make memories, ones that should have been ours.

"Ha ha." I heard Parker laugh, and a loud plop fill the air. I walked down the hallway and peeked into the spare bedroom.

"What's that?" I pointed to the box Parker sat next

to, pulling out papers.

"You saved all of these?" He shuffled through more folded notes from high school.

"I saved everything. Every note passed in school. Every letter sent during basic training and deployments, before video chat became a thing." I sat next to him and tucked my legs underneath me. Riffling through the box, I found tons of old pictures. "I saved pictures too. I haven't looked at these in forever, but I thought someday maybe our kids would like to see them." I sucked in my breath. "But that won't happen now."

Parker didn't say anything or even look at me. It seemed he was in denial of what was happening between us, or just didn't care. Either was totally plausible.

"Wow. This is the first note I ever wrote you. I remember Emily complaining that I didn't just call you."

He opened the letter, and I sat and listened to him read it out loud

Hey, Rainey,

I was hoping that you'd get to know me first before I showed you things about me that I'm not proud of. My life isn't all rainbows and butterflies and dreams of going to college. It's about surviving, wondering if I'll have dinner tonight, or a warm bed to sleep in.

At this point you've met Emily, my sixteen-year-old little sister who's pregnant by Adam. I shouldn't have touched him, but he hits her, so I figured I'd show him what a man hitting another man feels like. I know you're probably sitting there feeling sorry for me and Emily. She can dish it out as good as she gets it, don't let her fool you. And me, well you saw what I can do.

I'm a scrapper. I do what needs to be done in order to survive. I wear a ROTC uniform because the army is the only way I know how to get out of my current situation and start my own life. College isn't an option for me like it is you. You're smart. I can see it. Plus, I may have asked around about you.

I have no idea why I'm telling you all this. Maybe so there's full disclosure between us? I don't know. You don't owe me anything, but from the moment I saw you at the diner, I knew I'd see you again. So, you know what I did? I walked out and threw away your number, and here I am, at your school.

I'll be back in school tomorrow. Here's a number to reach me. In case you can't wait that long.

See you tomorrow.

Always,

Parker

We sat in silence for a moment just taking in the letter.

"I sure had a way with words, didn't I?" Parker chucked the letter back into the box. I didn't know why he was getting so angry all of a sudden.

Bringing my legs close to my chest, I answered. "You did. It was one of the reasons why I fell in love with you. Your words were magical."

He snickered. "My fucked-up past offset that. My anger destroyed my love for words and sent me straight into the army. Now look."

I stretched out and thought about what he said. I was looking, right at a man whose life could have ended up just like his sister's. Our marriage might be ending, but what his life could have been was a lot worse.

"If you think of where you could have ended up, this is a much better alternative." I tried to offer a reassuring smile.

"You always encouraged me, even when I was an asshole, which was more often than not. Thank you for that. For believing in me when I didn't believe in myself." He fiddled with the outside of the box, avoiding my eyes. "I'm sorry I couldn't love you the way you needed. The way you deserved. I hope someone comes along and makes you forget all about the shit I put you through." He finally stopped picking at the box and looked up at me, tears glistening in his eyes. "I'm so sorry for failing you. For failing us."

My heart was crushed. Parker was damaged, much

more so than I ever imagined. Our life didn't turn out how we planned, but all of this was making me stronger, wiser, and more in tune with who I was as an individual. So much of my identity had been tied to Parker since finding him at such a young age. I lost parts of myself when I fell in love with him. I was finally becoming the person I was destined to be. But as much as it was wonderful to know that I was healing, becoming whole, and I knew I was going to be better because of this divorce, Parker was hurting, and despite our marriage not working, I wouldn't just give up on him.

"Oh, Parker." I brought him in for a hug. It wasn't a quick embrace; it was long, full of all the emotions that we had battled with for years. I felt all his fears, hesitations, and struggles, and it damn near broke me. "It's going to be okay. Life has a funny way of working itself out."

"How can you forgive me?" He wiped his tears on his shirt. "I cheated on you because I was too weak to put in the effort that our marriage needed to survive. You did everything for me, and I let that all go because I thought something shiny and new wouldn't make the demons I face every day as real. That maybe someone else wouldn't notice. I was an asshole husband, and you still find it in you to comfort me like I didn't do anything wrong."

I thought about the spot I was in a few weeks ago, drowning myself in ice cream and tears. I hadn't forgiven him then, I never thought I could. I was angry that he threw away our dreams for someone else, but it all made sense now. People grow apart. Even epic first love like Parker and I had.

"I knew we were meant to be from the first moment I saw you in that diner. I made the mistake of assuming that meant forever. That we'd grow old together, raise kids, and sit on our porch sipping coffee chatting about the good old days. That we'd look forward to our grandkids coming over for sleepovers, and I'd bake cookies, and we'd give them too much sugar then send them home. But forever isn't always in the cards. I know that these past years were meant to be. We were meant to cross paths and guide each other to this point. I've learned so much from you, Parker. What I gained from you, how to live in high school when all I was obsessed with was my GPA and books, how to kiss, how to make love... those are the things that will stick with me forever. Those are the parts that I'll always cherish." I took a breath. "So, forgiving you is a small price to pay to know that the lessons you taught me will be with me forever. I wish you all the best in your life, and I will be here for you—always. We have something many people can't say they have, first love."

"Jesus, and you struggled with writing in high school?" Parker laughed. "You're amazing, Rainey. Some guy will be lucky to have you someday. I hope he's everything I wasn't."

"And I hope she's everything I'm not," I whispered.

Silence hung in the air. Promises that weren't kept. Love that was lost.

"Where do we go from here?" Parker asked as he stood.

"We live."

CHAPTER THIRTEEN

After the conversation with Parker, I felt free. Lighter, happier. We talked until the sun came up and then went into our separate bedrooms. There was no more animosity between us, or hate, which made it a bit easier. Hate could weigh you down, and I hadn't realized how angry and hate-filled I had been until I let some of it go.

My cell phone buzzed, and I realized I hadn't checked it since yesterday when Parker and I had our heart-to-heart.

It was Ava. I answered the phone and prepared myself for an earful.

"Bitch, listen here, I've been texting you since last night. You better have screwed Levi and been passionately in his embrace all night long; otherwise, I'm mad at you and will never forgive you for not answering my messages."

I laughed. "No, I was with Parker. He flew in yesterday." I listened to her drop something in the background.

"You didn't? Please tell me you didn't get back together with him!" Her voice was low, the tone she reserved for scolding her children.

"No. We just talked, reminisced. It was good. I needed it. He needed it."

"He needs a quick kick to the nuts for cheating on you. That's what he needs," Ava added. "But I'm glad you talked it out. I'm sure it's easier to be friends and part ways on good terms than hate each other's guts. Although it would have been great for him to come home to all his shit out on the front lawn."

I rolled my eyes. Ava and her dramatics. "While I'm not sure if that would have been the most mature reaction, I can see how it would have been therapeutic." I giggled.

"So, Levi. What happened? Did you kiss? Did you bone? Please give me something juicy. I need to live vicariously through you. I have to schedule sex with Beckett like it's my annual pap smear. Give me details, woman!"

"No details to give. He saved me from another depression-induced romance movie and Ben and Jerry's session. We went to the beach. No funny business. I'm not ready for any of that."

"Boring," Ava said with a fake snore. "Did he at least try? He so wants you, doesn't he?" I could hear the smile in her voice.

"I told him I couldn't kiss him."

"Why the hell not?" she screeched.

"I'm trying not to jump from one relationship to another. Shouldn't I take time to be alone? To figure out where I go from here?" It was a rhetorical question. Were there rules on how soon after you decided to divorce your husband that you moved on? There had to be a rule book or something.

"You are falling into your old ways. Not everything has rules and needs a life plan. Let things happen as they should. Don't deny yourself a fun time because you feel like you must follow some rules that don't exist. You aren't cheating."

"I know that," I countered.

"Then what are you afraid of?"

Everything? Opening myself up to someone, even if just for a friendship that could hurt me. When you suffer from depression, so much is a potential to exacerbate the outbursts. With Parker, it was easier to stay home and veg because of our lifestyle, but now, if I had any hope of living again, I had to get out there, and it was terrifying and exciting all at the same time.

I glanced up as Parker appeared in the doorway, dressed and ready to head to the hospital to see Emily.

"All right, Ava, I got to go. Time to go see Emily. I won't ever ignore your messages again. I'm sorry, and I love you."

"Apology accepted. Love you, and tell Parker I said

to drop dead." The phone went silent.

"Ava says hi," I said to Parker as I shoved my phone in my purse and headed toward the door.

He let out a small laugh. "Sure, she did."

"You ready?" I held the door open. "She's not doing well."

"I'm as ready as I'll ever be. Sometimes it's best to just go for it and not think about it too much."

I nodded and locked the door behind us. I knew his words were meant regarding Emily, but they made sense to me on other levels too. I was an overthinker, and sometimes you just had to let go.

***

I'd never seen Parker so on edge. His jaw clenched as he listened to Emily and the therapist speak. I sat and listened, their childhood the topic of conversation and how much it had impacted Emily. Parker had shared most of his past with me, it was inevitable with how long we'd been together, but hearing it from Emily's mouth, watching the tears stream down her face as she spoke of the abuse, losing herself in mindless sex, giving up a child for adoption... it hurt my heart.

"Do you regret giving up your child for adoption?" Marcie, the therapist, probed. It was a difficult topic that never got mentioned around Emily. I watched Emily's shoulders tense, and I wanted to scream at Marcie. What a stupid question.

"Of course, it impacted her," Parker said, leaning forward. "I don't understand how dredging up all of this past shit is going to help. Let's focus on getting Emily clean. A fresh start. That's what she needs, not sitting here and bringing up a past that we can't change. We had a screwed-up childhood. Big deal!" His jaw clenched, as did his fist as he leaned back into the chair. I reached out and squeezed his knee, trying to offer him some semblance of comfort. With a swift shift of his leg, he brushed me away.

Why the hell am I here?

"Our childhoods shape who we are. Whether we want to remember or not, they are all very much a part of us. Emily's addiction and her promiscuous tendencies all can be linked to her childhood." Marcie placed down her pen. Parker was a tough sell on anything to do with mental health. He did the bare minimum that the army required. He believed that drinking water, working out, and eating healthy could cure just about anything. So this was extremely out of his element.

"Bullshit." He shook his head. "I can't do this." He stood up, jarring the table with his leg.

"You never could. That's why you left. Run away, big brother. Run away from the shitty life we had. Pretend it never happened. Run away from your marriage. That's what you do. I don't run."

"No, you fucking shoot up and spread your legs." Parker's voice was low, the vibration shaking me to my core. His anger was showing, the same anger that had made me keep my mouth shut for so many years. Emily didn't play that game, though. She never cowered from him. Ever.

"Now, settle down. We don't place blam—" Marcie tried to bring order back to her session.

"Classic Parker. Points at all that is wrong with his baby sister, but won't look at himself. Look at this woman." She pointed to me. "She's beautiful. She worshipped the ground you walked on so much it made me sick, and you cheated on her. Seems like I'm not the only one with fucking problems." She laughed and crossed her legs.

And it just got even more awkward. Why was I being brought into this? I felt like I was at a tennis match watching these two go at it, and now they threw me in to make an already shitty situation worse. Parker paced the office, making it seem even smaller with his large frame.

"Rainey, you've been awfully quiet over there." Marcie gave me a small smile.

"I feel like I shouldn't be here," I stated. "This is family business, and I'm—"

"Not family anymore." Parker's eyes bore into me. He was like Dr. Jekyll and Mr. Hyde. One moment he was having a heart-to-heart with me over old letters, and the next he was slicing me with his words. I'd been sliced enough to last a lifetime. I was surprised I didn't bleed out.

"Exactly." I squared my shoulders, trying to sound

stronger than I felt, and bit back the tears.

"See!" Emily flung up her hands. "He's pushing away one of the only other people who believes in me, who has stuck by me through all of this, because he's damaged too. At least I admit I have a problem."

"This isn't about me!" Parker leaned up against the wall, crossing his arms over his chest.

"No. It's about all of you. How Emily's addiction, and all that's happened, has changed each of you and directly impacted your lives. Addiction doesn't just touch the user, it impacts the entire family." Marcie tapped her pen against the yellow notebook that she had been writing in the entire session. I fought the urge to scoot closer to read what she was writing. How fucked-up were we? "Emily, tell Parker what he means to you. Tell him what you told me."

Emily shifted in her chair and looked over at me. I gave her a reassuring nod. Sometimes just laying it all out there was the best way with Parker. He understood direct best. I tended to be more passive-aggressive, which didn't work well.

"You're my fucking brother. You protected me from beatings, made sure I never went to bed hungry when Mom and Dad would be out doing God knows what. Who I am, the choices I made, aren't because of what you didn't do for me, because you did everything. I just wanted—" Her voice cracked. "I want to be different. I don't want to be like Mom, but here I am, her fucking spitting image. But it's all I've known, and you stick with what you know." Silent tears streamed down Emily's face. Parker slowly moved toward her and took her in his arms. He stroked her hair, his voice shaking with emotion that caused tears to stream down my face.

"I didn't do enough. I ran. I left you here and didn't think about how not having me around would influence you. I failed you as a brother."

Emily squirmed from his embrace and looked between him and me. "You both are constantly there for me whenever I screw up. If it wasn't for you both, I'd be dead. Your love for each other gave me hope." Reaching over to me, Emily took my hand in hers and squeezed.

I thought my marriage was a fail, that the past years of my life meant nothing, but looking into Emily's eyes, I knew it was exactly what it needed to be.

CHAPTER FOURTEEN

Everything that happened with Emily, our confessions, the therapy session, really helped. Therapy wasn't a magic cure, but when you knew the feelings of the other people involved, where they stood and what they truly thought of you, it could make some of the challenges easier.

Parker and I spent the days he had stateside packing up the house that we once shared and laughing like old times. The tension between us wasn't as poignant; we had made a silent agreement to let the past be the past and focus on the here and now. We visited Emily daily for more therapy sessions, some of which I was a part of, and others I stayed behind. Whatever was happening behind those closed doors was good for them both. Parker seemed lighter, maybe even happier. Emily was doing better, and me? Well, I would get there. It was hard closing a chapter of my life that I thought was already written, watching a family that I was once a part of slowly becoming something without me.

I curled up to read a book on the sofa. Reading was an escape. I could live in someone else's world for as long as I wanted. It made all that was around me disappear and offered a respite from all that was going on. Even though things were difficult, I knew that things that provided us with the most grief brought us the most growth, and I'd grown through this experience. I couldn't wait to see all that I'd become from this.

"Hey." Parker walked into the living room and sat across from me on the couch. "I have the paperwork here for the divorce." My heart twisted in my chest. Parker didn't even pay any bills, but I guess when you really wanted something you figured out a way, huh?

"Oh?" I took the papers from his hands and read. Standard divorce paperwork where there was no contest between parties. Everywhere I needed to sign was nicely pointed out with sticky notes.

"I figured we didn't need to get lawyers involved. We have to be living apart for a year for it to be official. I still have time left on this tour, and I'm due for reenlistment, so I figured just get it started now." Parker rubbed his head. He didn't seem to be emotional in the least.

Reaching over to the side table, I grabbed a pen and clicked it open. I placed the papers on the table and signed.

"Guess that's it, huh? Eight years over with a signature." I handed him the signed papers.

He stood up, and I caught a hint of the young boy I fell in love with. His face didn't hold all the pain of his past that haunted him. I wanted to make it all go away. To love him so much that the pain was nothing but a distant memory. But I couldn't. You couldn't love someone if they didn't want to be loved. You couldn't make them forget if all they wanted to do was hold on.

"Eight years. We had some good times." He smiled. "Like vacationing in the Bahamas. Remember the waterfall?"

"I remember. There isn't much I don't remember." I did remember it all, every good and bad memory.

Parker's eyes softened. "This will be good for us. You'll see." His phone rang in his pocket. "It's Samantha. I better get it."

"Of course. Sure." I sat up in the chair and plastered a smile on my face. He had Samantha. He'd moved on before we were even over and found what he needed in someone else. While I wished I had someone to comfort me, I knew that I'd lost so much of myself in my marriage. I gave my all, not leaving anything for me. I didn't want to do that again, but that was easier said than done. I gave my all in everything I did in life. As a nurse, I got overly attached to my patients. My friendships lasted forever because the thought of starting over scared me shitless. I clung to what I knew.

It was easier than the unknown.

My cell danced on the table, and an incoming message from Levi flitted across the screen. I hadn't spoken to him since Parker came back. There I was again, putting my all into something and not finding balance.

Levi: Pizza? Movie? Tomorrow?

Me: Sure. After 5 works for me. Parker leaves tomorrow early afternoon.

Levi: Ah. Is everything going okay with that? I can beat him up if you want.

The thought of Levi and Parker going at it made me giggle. Parker would kick Levi's ass, but the fact that he was willing, even if joking, was funny.

Me: Appreciate the offer, but we're good. Things are good.

Levi: That's good. I'm glad you guys are working things out.

Shit. He'd misread my message.

Me: No. Not making things work. Just in a better spot. We just signed divorce paperwork.

The three dots that showed when someone was messaging back danced on the screen for longer than I cared to see. Was he writing an epic novel?

Levi: Okay. See you tomorrow.

I didn't know what I expected him to say, but when you saw those three dots for so long, you expected something more profound. Frustrated, I didn't even reply. I picked my book back up and got lost in a made-up world, because currently, it seemed much better than mine.

CHAPTER FIFTEEN

I pulled up to the airport and managed to find a spot amongst the chaos of drop-offs and pickups. I usually parked and walked into the airport, waiting until the absolute last second to say goodbye to Parker, but things were different now.

"I guess this is it." Parker's hand hovered over the car door handle. He opened the door, and the weight of everything crushed my chest. I hated goodbyes. I hated this goodbye. The finality of it was heart-wrenching.

"Keep in touch?" I questioned, clutching the steering wheel between my hands.

"Yeah. Take care of yourself, Rainey."

"Keep your head down."

"I always do." And with a slam of the door, my husband of the past eight years was gone. I watched him walk away, torturing myself until the absolute last second. I felt like I was losing pieces of myself with each step he took. I'd been wrapped up in him since I was seventeen years old, and now I had to figure out who the hell I was without him. I had no fucking clue.

A slap on my window startled me.

"Move along, please." An annoying security guard glared at me through the window. I smiled sweetly and pulled away from the curb, away from everything I'd ever known.

***

I was weak when I wanted to be strong. I was soft when I wanted to be fierce. I never knew when an episode would hit me. When all the things I had to be happy for would melt away like snow in the summer. Today was one of the days where nothing could bring me out of the slump.

After leaving the airport, I tried to call Ava, and it went straight to voice mail. That started the downward spiral that was my day.

My own expectations hurt me. The expectation that I was going to be loved and married for the rest of my life. That babies, a house, and a dog were in my near future. My own expectations ruined me.

Maybe that's why things were easier for those who just flew through life never expecting anything. But I threw myself into life and felt that if I put my all into everything I did, that there was no way life could screw me over. Well, I was wrong.

The thing with depression was that it could be crippling. It's just not something that lingers in your brain, you could feel in your bones, throughout your skin. It traveled and showed no mercy when it took over. It turned every positive thing in your life into a disaster. It made you forget about everyone who loved and cared for you. It ruined you from the inside out.

I clung to my wet clothes as I sat in the shower; the water had turned cold forever ago. I couldn't even undress. I was numb. In a daze that I couldn't get out of. I'd thought I had myself together, that I accepted everything that was happening. I signed the damn divorce papers. I sat in therapy sessions and felt happy.

Depression showed no mercy.

"Rainey? Are you in here? I tried to call you. Your door was unlocked. I just wanted to make sure you were okay." I heard Levi's voice, but I couldn't move. I was frozen. Unable to find the words to tell him where I was.

"Rainey? Please answer me." I heard him drop something on the counter, his footsteps getting louder and louder. I heard a knock at the bathroom door. "Rainey. I'm coming in."

I looked up just as the door to the bathroom opened. I didn't even care what he saw, because this was me. The real me. I was scared of what lurked in the ocean. I was scared of losing myself again. I hated fucking pepperoni on my pizza. I was lost. I had been for some time.

"Jesus," Levi mumbled as he snatched the towel down from where it hung. He turned off the water. Wrapping me up, he took me in his arms.

"Stop. You'll get all wet," I whispered.

"Shh. Stop worrying about everyone else for a minute and let me take care of you." I looked up and straight into his blue eyes. He brushed the matted, wet hair away from my face and smiled down at me. "Let me help you."

I didn't want to be helped. I wanted to sit here and wallow in my own misery until my limbs were so cold that I couldn't feel anything. That would be easier than the disappointment that washed over me. But there was something in Levi's eyes, something in his voice that made the cold water disappear and warmth travel over me.

"Okay," I agreed.

"Good. Now let's get you changed and warm, and you can tell me all about what happened." He stood up from beside me next to the tub. His entire chest was soaked, the shirt he wore clinging to his body.

"I brought pizza."

My stomach growled at his words. Levi laughed.

"I hope just cheese is okay. I remember you said you didn't like pepperoni, but I wasn't sure what you liked."

Levi helped me out of the tub, and I stopped and stared at him.

"What?" he asked, tilting his head to the side.

I remembered Parker forgetting I hated pepperoni and telling me to pretty much suck it up. It felt awful to have someone who was supposed to know everything about you disregard you. It was something simple, but it still stung.

"You remembered. You listened." Tears streamed down my face.

"I listen to everything you say, Rainey." Levi brought me in for a hug, and although he was covered in water, it warmed me.

"I'm sorry he hurt you," he whispered.

"It wasn't his fault. It was my own expectations. I expect too much from people." I wiped away my tears and pulled the towel closer against my body.

The fire in Levi's eyes startled me. "Stop that. Stop selling yourself short. Your expectations are what they should be. Whatever you want, you need, you desire, you should have. Never expect anything else, and don't make excuses for what he put you through."

I had no words after he said that, so I settled for a gentle nod. Levi had come into my life at the worst time. He was seeing me at my worst, and I didn't know why he was still here. If I were him, I would have run away from the craziness that I was the first day I jumped down his throat. Instead, he pulled me from the depths of my mind and held me when I needed someone the most.

"I'm going to go change. I think Parker left a few things behind in the spare room. You can put something dry on." I pointed him in the direction he needed to go.

"Thanks." I watched as he walked down the hall, the wet shirt clinging to his toned back. I took a second to compose myself and get my thoughts as right as I could, and then I went to change.

I opted for something comfortable, a pair of my favorite sweatpants and a T-shirt. Right now, I just wanted to be surrounded by things that were comfortable and didn't require much effort. My mind was still a bit fuzzy, but Levi had mostly snapped me out of it. At least for now.

I headed into the kitchen to plate the pizza. Levi cleared his throat behind me, and I turned around. He had on a pair of gray sweatpants and a black T-shirt. Huh. I didn't remember those on Parker. There was something about a man in gray sweatpants. It was like lingerie.

"These are a little big." Levi spread out his arms and pulled on the waist of the pants.

"Parker's a muscly guy," I commented as I turned around and pulled down two plates.

"I'll still fight him." Placing the plates on the counter, Levi grinned ear to ear.

That managed to coax a smile out of me. "Let's eat," I said.

We sat in silence, eating our pizza. Levi reached over me to grab another slice and grazed my chest with his arm. Nothing could prepare me for how I felt, the excitement that coursed through my body that just minutes before was chilled to the bone. I shivered.

"You're cold. Want a sweater?" Levi asked.

"I'm fine." I shoved more pizza in my mouth and tried to focus on anything but what I'd just felt. I was confused, trying to forget my failed marriage, and Levi was here and available. That's all it was. I need to simmer the hell down before I ruined my life any more than it already was. Our friendship was more important than whatever my libido had in mind. Even if him remembering that I hated pepperoni was sexy as hell.

CHAPTER SIXTEEN

I was thankful to be at work. There was nothing like a twelve-hour shift in the chaos that was the ER to make me forget about everything. I stretched, mentally readying myself for work.

"I'm so sorry to hear about you and Parker." Jean gave me a hug.

"Wow, news travels fast, huh?" I tried to laugh it off, but it bothered me. Now, the solace of my job would become filled with endless I'm sorrys and what happened. This was supposed to be my safe place, my place to escape.

"Well, you aren't wearing your ring." Jean glanced down at my ring finger that was bare, except for a faint outline from all the years that my wedding band had been there. I had forgotten I took it off the day Parker told me he had been seeing someone else.

"Right," I said as Jean and I walked together. I

snagged a chart from outside the curtain of the next patient in the ER.

"I know we aren't really close, but I'm here if you ever want to talk. I got divorced a year ago. It isn't easy, but you'll be better for it." Jean teared up.

"Really?" I realized how little I knew about the people I worked with. Another part of my life I kept my distance from.

"Yeah. We weren't together as long as you and Parker, but I thought he was my forever. Guess life had other plans." Jean laughed. "I'm good now. Took a while, but I moved on. I have Craig, and I'm happy. Really happy."

"That's good, Jean. I'm happy for you, but I'm not ready to date. The ink hasn't even dried on my divorce papers yet."

Jean put her hands on both my shoulders. "I never thought I'd be ready either, but Craig came into my life, and it was perfect." Her eyes averted to the side as Levi walked down the hall, smiling at me. Jean winked at me before she scurried away, leaving me and the incoming Levi.

"Hey," I said, clutching the chart in my hand. "I was just about to go in and see this patient."

"Cool. I just dropped someone off and wanted to see if I could take you out to dinner tonight?" Levi ran his fingers through his hair and shifted from foot to foot. I liked that he was slightly nervous asking me to dinner, because I was nervous too, about everything. The past.

The future. Life. I was a walking anxiety attack waiting to happen.

"I'd love to, but I work until 7:00 a.m." I clutched the chart even tighter, my fingers going numb.

"Oh. That's cool. No worries, maybe another time." He shoved his hands in his pockets.

"How about breakfast?" I smiled wide. "I love french toast."

"Yeah. That sounds good. The diner across the street work?"

"Sounds good, Levi. And thanks for the other night. If you weren't there…."

"Hey." He leaned forward and tucked a strand of hair behind my ear that had fallen from my ponytail. "Don't mention it."

It was hard not to mention the intimate nature of what we shared that night. He'd held me in my most vulnerable state and didn't walk away. He showed me more care than my husband of eight years ever did. I wanted to mention it because it meant something to me, more than he'd ever know.

"I've got to get going before I get fired. Tomorrow. Breakfast. The diner." I gave him a thumbs-up before going behind the curtain and getting my shift started. I wasn't exactly sure what tomorrow would bring, but french toast and coffee? I could look forward to that.

***

I was exhausted. Working twelve hours and heading right to breakfast wasn't the smartest choice. I wanted to curl up in my bed, pull the curtains tight, and sleep until my shift tonight.

"What are you thinking about?" I opened my eyes, and Levi stared at me, humor dancing in his eyes. "Looks like whatever it is, you're enjoying."

"My bed. No offense, this was great, but twelve hours is killer, especially in the ER on a Friday night." I stuffed another piece of french toast in my mouth.

"I know what that's like. I'm off the next few days, though, so I'll miss the craziness of the weekend for a change." Levi took a sip of his tea. It still astounded me that he didn't drink coffee, especially in our line of work. Coffee was my lifeline.

I looked out the window that highlighted the beautiful day. The sun was shining, birds were chirping, and I smiled.

"You're full of expressive faces this morning. Care to let me in on what's making you smile? Not that I'm complaining, because I love your smile. It's nice to see you happy."

I looked at Levi thoughtfully. Was I happy? I wasn't so sure what happy was anymore. I'd had ebbs and flow of happiness all throughout my life, but how I felt right now, content, even remotely satisfied, could have been the french toast, or it could have been something more.

"It's just a beautiful day. The sun's out. I just ate

french toast in good company. I don't want it to end."

Levi put his cup of tea down and signaled the waitress for the check. "The day doesn't have to end. Let's go to the park."

I laughed. "The park?"

"Sure. Lots of fun things to do at the park."

Screw it. What did I have to lose but a couple of hours of sleep?

"I'm going to need a coffee to go." With a smile, Levi paid the check and ordered me a coffee to go and himself a tea.

***

Who knew playing in the park as an adult was so much fun? It was still early, so Levi and I were the only ones. It was peaceful, swinging on the swings as the sun kissed my cheeks.

"Want to go make out under the play scape?"

I gaped at the frankness of Levi's words. He wiggled his eyebrows. "Levi!" I said with a laugh.

"I'm teasing. Unless you want to help me fulfill that fantasy? I won't object." He pumped his legs and swung a little higher, having to raise his voice so I could hear him.

"That's your fantasy? Making out under the play scape?" I twisted around on the swing like I used to when I was younger.

Levi stopped himself from swinging and hopped off.

I watched him stalk toward me like a dog after a bone. His eyes, the brightness of them, turned darker, like a storm was brewing. Placing his hands on the ropes of my swing, he knelt so he was at eye level with me.

"If you haven't figured it out yet, Raindrop, anything that includes you is a fantasy of mine, but I know you're hurting and struggling, and I would never pursue you until you're ready. So, until that day, I'll take you out, wrap you in towels when you feel like you just can't go on, and I'll prove to you that not all guys are assholes and cheat."

Instinctively, I licked my lips. Everything was telling me to press my lips against his. I wanted to feel again, to take a leap of faith without fear. To think about myself for once and what I wanted, and right now, I wanted Levi.

"Don't lick your lips like that. I meant what I said. I'm waiting until you tell me you're ready, but I don't think you know how hard it's been to watch you struggle. I've fought to keep my distance. I don't want to start what I know will be something amazing between us due to some sexual attraction, or a need for you to escape. I want you to mean it, because I sure as hell will."

Levi stood up, releasing his hands from the swing, sending me spinning. Closing my eyes, I let his words take me over. He wanted me. He'd wait for me until I was ready. I was attracted to him and knew he was a good guy, but something he'd said stuck with me.

I shouldn't try to screw away the memories of Parker, and I wouldn't, because something told me that what Levi and I might share could be worth the wait.

CHAPTER SEVENTEEN

Zombie status. I was on autopilot. Giving report for the last of my four shifts never felt so good. Well, maybe not as good as sleep. Oh, sweet sleep. I wiped my chin where I swore some drool had already fallen.

"Rainey Matthews?" I squinted my bloodshot eyes and saw a man in front of me holding a dozen roses and a large coffee from the diner across the street.

"That's me." He gave me something to sign, and I took the flowers. Jean and a few of the other ladies from the shift came over.

"Who are those from?" Jean smiled widely.

"No clue. But there's coffee." I took a sip and moaned. Jean snatched the card and read it out loud. "Hey!"

"Raindrop, I just wanted you to know I was thinking about you. I know your addiction to caffeine, so I'm sure the coffee will make you happier than the flowers.

Next time I'll just send a bouquet of Keurig pods. Yours, Levi." Jean held the card to her chest. "Well, isn't that the sweetest thing I've ever read."

I snatched the card from her hand and read the words with my own eyes. The fact that he was thinking about me, that he went through the effort of sending me flowers, meant more to me than all the coffee in the world.

"Are you guys dating?" Mary, another nurse, asked.

"We aren't anything but friends."

"Uh-hum. Sure. He wants to be more than friends. You better snatch him up before someone else does," Jean said with a wink. "All right, let's get back to work. New shift, start!"

Before heading home to pass out for the day, I pulled out my phone and sent Levi a text.

Me: **Thanks so much for the coffee. Oh, the flowers were nice too. How about dinner tonight at my place? I'll cook!**

I watched the three little dots dance across the screen.

Levi: **Sounds good. I'm out at 5. Let's say 7?**

Me: **Perfect.**

Gathering my flowers and coffee, I had a bit of extra energy. It'd been a while since someone did something for me like Levi did. It was a good start to a new day and a new life.

*** *** ***

I managed a solid three hours of sleep before I stared at the ceiling, trying to figure out what I was going to make for dinner. I wasn't a horrible cook, but I lived on simple and easy, especially with Parker being gone all the time. Salads, frozen Healthy Choice meals, and sometimes I just ate a protein bar and called it a day.

I settled for something easy and less likely for me to burn. Spaghetti, garlic bread, and salad. I prepped everything and then focused on myself. Levi had seen me more in my scrubs than anything else; tonight I wanted to make an effort. He'd tried since the first day I met him, and that was refreshing, to have someone care enough to send flowers and find out how I liked my coffee. To listen when I said I hated pepperoni on my pizza. Those things mattered to me, and I was happy to finally have met someone who valued that.

My cell rang, and I put it on speaker so I could chat with Ava and put on some makeup.

"What's up? I feel like I haven't spoken to you in forever," Ava said as she munched on something.

"We spoke yesterday, and what the hell are you eating? It's so loud."

"Stupid carrots. I'm just a girl standing in front of a carrot, asking it to be a damn piece of chocolate cake." Ava groaned. "I hate dieting."

"Then don't diet. Balance."

"Okay, Obi-Wan. What are you doing? I sound like I'm on speaker." I pulled my hair back so I could see my face to apply eyeliner.

"Currently putting on eyeliner." I stabbed myself in the eye, sending tears streaming down my face. Taking a piece of toilet paper, I dabbed my eye and started over. "Or trying to."

"Oh shit! You have a date."

"Mommy, you said bad word," I heard Amelia, one of Ava's daughters, say in the background.

"I did. Don't listen to Mommy," Ava said.

"I invited Levi over for dinner. Get this, he sent me flowers and a coffee this morning after my shift."

"Girl—" Another loud crunch sounded in my ear. "—he's amazing. Tell me he has some flaw?"

I managed to get a thin line of eyeliner on my eye. I didn't wear makeup much. In my line of work, simple was best. By the end of a shift, I'd look like a raccoon anyway if I applied too much cosmetics.

"Nothing that I know of. I'm sure there's something. It'll reveal itself in due time."

"Maybe he has a small pecker," Ava suggested.

"Mommy, what's a pecker?"

I laughed. "You better watch it, Amelia will be walking around talking about peckers at three years old."

"She said fuck the other day. In the correct context. Pretty sure Beckett and I aren't winning parent of the year anytime soon."

I applied a neutral color to my eyelids and pink gloss to my lips while Ava and I continued to chat. I still looked natural, just enhanced, which was what I liked for myself anyway. I wasn't one of those women to bother with contouring and changing the shape of my nose and cheeks. I didn't know how if I wanted to, anyway.

"Just be careful, okay, sweetie? I want you to be happy, but sometimes your…."

"I know my depressive moods come out of nowhere. Levi has already seen that side of me, and he didn't run away. That's saying something."

Ava sighed. "It is. It really is."

The doorbell rang, interrupting our conversation.

"Shit. He's here." I fumbled to throw all my makeup in the drawer to make the bathroom look less of a mess.

Ava laughed. "Have fun. Use protection, and I hope his pecker isn't small."

"Pecker! Pecker!" Amelia repeated in the background.

"Jesus, Ava." I laughed. "Chat later. Love you."

"Love you too."

With a deep breath, I took one last look at myself. My simple jeans and tight red halter top hugged my body just right. I'd opted for flats over heels because my feet were still hurting from my four shifts. They probably would be until right before my next shift. Such was the life of a nurse.

"You can do this," I said out loud to myself. I opened

the door, and Levi stood there, one hand in his pocket, the other holding a bottle of wine.

"I wasn't sure what you drank, but you didn't strike me as a red wine girl, so I settled for white."

"It's perfect." I took it from his hand. "Come in." I walked toward the kitchen with Levi following.

"I hope you don't mind spaghetti. It was the easiest, and I knew I wouldn't burn it."

"Spaghetti is perfect. So, what can I do to help?" Levi washed his hands in the sink. It was like he was comfortable in my kitchen, making himself right at home. For some that might have been disconcerting, but for me, it brought comfort. I didn't do awkward well, I didn't know many people who did, and having been out of the dating game for so long, I worried how I would do with all the preliminary things, the getting-to-know-you phase that always seemed to reveal so much about a person. I was getting to know Levi, and so far, like Ava said, it seemed like he had no flaws.

"Want to open the wine? I hate the popping sound it makes. The opener is in the drawer to the left."

Flashing me his dashing smile, he nodded. "You got it."

I poured the pasta into the boiling water, stealing glances of Levi as he opened the wine bottle. His toned arms strained against his plain white T-shirt—my weakness.

"You enjoying the view?" Levi grinned as the cork popped out. I shut my mouth that apparently had been hanging open.

I blushed, averting my eyes from his.

Levi poured two glasses of wine and handed me one.

"I like that you were checking me out because it shows that you're interested in me. Well, at least in my incredible muscles." He flexed and pretended he was posing for a bodybuilding competition.

I brought the wine glass to my lips. "You're right, I am interested, but like a fine wine, time makes it all better. The attraction between us just grows, and once we get together, it'll be explosive." I took a sip of the wine, grinning ear to ear. Levi placed his glass down and positioned his arms behind him to hold himself up on the counter. He smiled.

"That was the hottest thing I've ever heard," Levi said as he looked me up and down.

Turning around, I grabbed a noodle from the pot and chucked it against the wall.

Levi ducked, and I giggled.

"What are you doing?" he asked, looking at the noodle attached to the wall.

"That's how you check to see if it's done. If it sticks, it's ready."

"Huh?" he said. "Learn something new every day. Let me try!" Giddy, he ran to the pot and took out a noodle and threw it. Looking at me, he smiled.

This was what I wanted. The simple things. Cooking dinner together and living life with someone you cared about. There was so much that people took for granted, but I never would, not when I never had it.

"What?" he questioned, tilting his head to the side.

"This is nice, that's all. Cooking dinner with you." I strained the noodles, the steam from the hot water surrounding me.

"I'm glad, Raindrop," Levi said, bringing the two plates over to me. "Because this is only the beginning."

Trying to fight back my shit-eating grin, I hoped he was right, because this was what I had been waiting for.

CHAPTER EIGHTEEN

I snorted and gripped my side at Levi's British accent. A few glasses of wine turned into emptying the entire bottle and getting into my stash. Two and a half bottles later, Levi was showing me his impressions.

"It's good, huh? I think I missed my calling in life to be an actor." Levi flopped down on the couch next to me.

"Nope. Pretty sure you would be a starving actor." The music switched to "Perfect" by Ed Sheeran, and I clapped my hands.

"Love this song." I hummed along.

Levi jumped up and reached out his hand for me. "May I have this dance?" He wiggled his eyebrows at me.

I wasn't a good dancer, but with a few glasses of wine in me, I felt like I could do anything and do it well. I placed my hand in Levi's, and he pulled me close, one hand falling to my waist.

The silliness, the accents, all were gone. It was just us and the music. I was hyperaware of his hands, that both now were positioned on my waist. His touch was foreign, different from what I had been used to, but it made me feel alive. Resting my head against his shoulder, I relished his touch, the closeness of our bodies. I inhaled, the scent of his aftershave still lingering on his neck. My eyes studied his long neck, the muscles that were pulsing as I brought my hand up to stroke it. The fear and hesitation were gone, and all I wanted to do was taste him, to feel Levi's lips against mine.

He looked down just as my hands cupped his cheeks.

"Rainey." The music hummed in the background, and nothing could make this moment more perfect. Levi stood still, hesitation lingering in his eyes as he searched my face. "You have to tell me what you want." His hands gripped my arms, as if at any second he was going to either push me away or crash his lips down on mine. All I had to do was tell him that I was ready, and the tension, it'd be gone. The buildup in my mind of what this kiss would mean would come to an end.

"I'm ready," I whispered, our lips only inches apart. The way his hands gripped my arms, I expected the kiss to be hard and fast. With a smile, Levi let go of my arms and softly caressed my cheek. He placed his hand behind my head, and with a subtle lean, his lips gently met mine. It was slow at first, our lips and bodies becoming aligned. My arms hung by my side, then grasped around his neck to strengthen the connection. His tongue lashed out, coaxing my lips open. I nipped at his lip, and he moaned.

Breathlessly we parted, both our lips swollen from the kiss. I wasn't thinking of my past, of the heartache that I felt not long ago, but of how much kissing Levi was worth the wait.

We stood in front of each other, the song switching over before either of us spoke, the intensity of what just happened still buzzing in the air.

"That was intense," Levi finally said.

"It was." I brushed my fingers against my lips and smiled.

"Stop smiling like that, Raindrop, or I won't be going home tonight." My lips formed a perfect O shape at his confession.

"Don't worry." He moved toward me and kissed my forehead. "Not tonight. That kiss was everything I knew it would be. Remember what I said, I'll wait until you're ready. For everything." I breathed a sigh of relief. While I knew I wanted to see where things would go with Levi, I wasn't ready to have sex with him yet. Although my wet panties would say otherwise, I wanted to take things slow. Relish the little things, like a first kiss that almost knocked me on my ass.

"On that note…." He glanced at his cell phone. "It's after midnight. I'm going to go home since I have to be up for work in six hours."

"Oh, here!" I rushed into the kitchen and swiped the container of food I had made him. "Take this home. You can have it for lunch tomorrow or whatever."

"Thank you." Levi pressed a kiss to my forehead as he held my front door open. Taking one last glance at me, he shook his head. "It's hard to go, but I know it's the right thing." I bit my lip and nodded. It was the right thing. Taking things slow, I reminded myself.

"Good night, Levi."

"Night, Raindrop." I latched the door behind him and flung myself on the couch.

"Holy shit!" I screeched. Everything about tonight was perfect. Nothing could take away the feelings of being wanted and cared for that I felt whenever Levi was around.

A knock at the door made me jump. I smiled, thinking that Levi couldn't leave.

"Levi, I thought we said we'd wait…." I opened the door, fully prepared to give myself to Levi, to strip down and make love to him, because I deserved that. I deserved to feel something again other than heartache. When I opened the door, my smile melted away. It wasn't Levi. In front of me stood Parker.

"Rainey."

I stumbled back and gripped the side of the door. "What are you doing here? Aren't you supposed to be in Afghanistan?" Parker looked me over, stopping at my face that still had makeup from my date with Levi.

I was suddenly extremely self-conscious. I pulled down my halter top.

"I'm done. I didn't go back. I was up for reenlistment and didn't sign. I'm out. I should have been out years ago when you begged me to stay and start a family. When you told me that this life wasn't what you wanted. I won't lie and say I haven't made mistakes. That I didn't run out on our marriage, but it was because I was weak. Damaged. Broken. And I still am. But my God, Rainey, falling in love with you at seventeen was the best thing that has ever happened to me. I can't throw that all away."

This couldn't be happening. Not here. Not now. After all these years of trying to get Parker to understand how this life was impacting me, he cheated on me, we filed for divorce, and now he wanted me to forgive him?

"I took a letter with me from the box you kept of all of our memories." He pulled a crinkled, grayed piece of lined paper out of his pocket and read.

"I forgot how beautiful the world was until I saw your face.

Your smile makes me forget all the pain.

Your touch brings me to a better place.

Chaos was my life until you calmed it.

Disaster was my soul until you mended it.

You saved me."

Tears streamed down my face. I ripped the letter from his hand and clutched it tightly. "But you broke me, Parker. You tore me into a million pieces. You stepped out on our marriage when I needed you the most."

Parker's own tears fell. "I'm sorry. I know that isn't enough. That these are just words. I'm going to get help. Finally see someone about my own issues. I promise you that I will spend the rest of our life together proving to you that I am the man you married eight years ago. I can fix this. We can fix this. Don't give up on us yet. Our story may have started when we were young, but it's going to continue forever. It has to." Parker fell to his knees, pulling me against him.

We wept together, standing in the doorway to what was once our home, the place where so many memories were made. The place where so many promises were broken.

What the fuck was I supposed to do?

THE END
For Now

Rainey, Levi, and Parker return in *Out of Goodbyes*.

ACKNOWLEDGMENTS

The Hopelessly Devoted series came into my head on the plane to my very first Romantic Times Convention. I sat on the plane and sent an email to Becky while in flight. I just want to thank you, Becky, for accepting my idea without reading it first and knowing where my sometimes (okay a lot of the time) crazy mind can take me.

I started writing this during the convention and had it mostly done before I left. Crazy, right? There is nothing like spending a week with some amazing people to have spark those creative juices!

Love you all and I promise the next installment is already on its way to you! Hang tight! There is a happily ever after in sight! Just bring tissues. You're in for a wild ride.

ABOUT THE AUTHOR

You can find Gen curled up reading paranormal romance and romantic thrillers or frantically typing her stories on her laptop.

Forensic psychology is her trade by day, teaching and molding the minds of college students. Her interest in psychology can be seen in her books, each including many psychological undertones. Although she loves teaching, her passion, her true love, lies in the stories that roam around in her head. Yes, they all come from her mind--the good, the bad, and the totally insane.

Gen Ryan is an international best-selling author in multiple sub genres within romance. She lives in Massachusetts--no, not Boston--with her husband, daughter, and American Eskimo dog named Chewbacca. With each story she shares, she hopes her love for writing and storytelling seeps through, encompassing the reader and leaving them wanting more.

Follow Gen:

FACEBOOK: WWW.FACEBOOK.COM/GENRYANAUTHOR

WEBSITE: WWW.GENRYANBOOKS.COM

TWITTER: TWITTER.COM/GENRYAN15

ABOUT THE PUBLISHER

Hot Tree Publishing opened its doors in 2015 with an aspiration to bring quality fiction to the world of readers. With the initial focus on romance and a wide spread of romance subgenres, we envision opening up to alternative genres in the near future.

Firmly seated in the industry as a leading editing provider to independent authors and small publishing houses, Hot Tree Publishing is the sister company to Hot Tree Editing, founded in 2012. Having established in-house editing and promotions, plus having a well-respected market presence, Hot Tree Publishing endeavors to be a leader in bringing quality stories to the world of readers.

Interested in discovering more amazing reads brought to you by Hot Tree Publishing or perhaps you're interested in submitting a manuscript and joining the HTPubs family? Either way, head over to the website for information:

WWW.HOTTREEPUBLISHING.COM

CPSIA information can be obtained
at www.ICGtesting.com
Printed in the USA
FFOW03n0055061117
43309344-41887FF